MW01595442

Finding Release

Wild R Farm Book 1

By Silvia Violet

Silvia Violet

Copyright © 2012 by Silvia Violet

Cover art by BitterGrace Art (©2012)

Edited by Liz Bichmann

First eBook edition July 2012
All Rights Reserved. No part of this eBook
may be used or reproduced in any manner
whatsoever without written permission except in
brief quotations embodied in critical articles or
reviews.

Finding Release is a work of fiction. Names, places,
characters, and incidents are either the product of
the author's imagination or are fictionalized. Any
resemblance to any actual persons, living or dead, is
entirely coincidental.

Dedication

To all those who rescue horses and patiently care for them.

Prologue

"That should be the last of it." Jonah tossed the final sack of feed on the back of Cole's truck parked outside his family's feed store. "You need anything else?"

Jonah looked at Cole with his big brown eyes as if he needed something. Cole caught his scent, and his wolf stirred to life. He smelled like horse and sweat with an underlying citrusy scent, young and clean. Prey. Cole's cock wanted to fulfill all Jonah's needs, but Cole wasn't stupid enough to even flirt with an eighteen-year-old high school senior whose stepfather had been the most vocally anti-gay preacher in town. The only reason the Marks family deigned to sell him grain was because in these hard times they needed his money.

Cole tried to ignore the fantasies playing out in his mind. "Nope. We're good."

Jonah looked down at his dusty boots. "You got a minute?"

Cole took a deep breath. He glanced around. They couldn't talk here, not openly. Jonah needed a friend, and Cole had once been young and different and scared. "Sure. You wanna get a cup of coffee?" He tilted his head toward the diner down the street.

"Yeah." Jonah looked at his watch. "I'm due for a break."

"All right. Mind if I leave the truck here?" Cole asked.

"Nah, we're not expecting another big delivery until this afternoon."

They walked to the diner in awkward silence.

Cole couldn't let himself think about how gorgeous Jonah looked, staring at him with those puppy dog eyes. Jonah was off limits for too many reasons to count.

They got a booth by the front windows, and Cole ordered coffee for them. Once the waitress brought the steaming mugs, Cole let himself look at Jonah. His red-brown hair was rumpled from finger combing. A combination of sunburn and embarrassment tinted his cheeks. His denim jacket hugged his broad shoulders and… No! Cole wasn't going to let his perusal go any lower, not even in his imagination. His wolf growled deep inside, his werewolf nature recognizing the equine inside Jonah, the shifter side his family forced him to deny.

He concentrated on Jonah's strong, pale hands as they wrapped around the coffee cup, holding it tight for warmth and stability. Cole wanted to reach out and take Jonah's hands in his own, but that would be bad for both of them.

Cole realized he'd made a mistake. He should have told Jonah he was in a hurry to get back to the farm, or something that would've kept him from sitting here alone with a very young horse shifter who was having an indescribable effect on him.

"Mr Wilder?"

Well, being addressed as 'Mister' certainly burst the lurid fantasy in his mind. He was only thirty, but now he felt ancient. "You know you can call me Cole."

Jonah's cheeks got even redder. "I know… it's just… I was wondering if you'd consider hiring me. I know I don't have experience working in a barn, but, I… well… I'm kind of a natural with horses." He grinned as he said this.

His cutely upturned mouth made him look even younger, and Cole cursed his inappropriate thoughts. The boy needed his help, not his perving.

Jonah's home life had to be hell. His father had left them when he was little, and his mother and elder brother were both self-righteous Bible-thumpers. From what he could tell, Jonah couldn't do a damn thing right in their eyes, but Jonah working at Wild R Farm would be a disaster. Cole could smell Jonah's desire for him. Sooner or later, he'd give into his own desire and exploit that. Jonah deserved freedom and a man who had more self-control.

Cole's wolf growled, the sound almost escaping Cole's mouth. If he put his hands on Jonah, he feared his wolfish instincts would take over. Jonah smelled like prey, like something to be consumed, possessed. Cole shuddered. No. He could never let those desires loose. "Jonah, I—"

"Please…" He dropped his voice to a whisper. "My family… I can't live with them anymore."

"Your mother's not going to let you work for me."

"I'm eighteen. She can't stop me."

Cole tried a different tactic. "You need to finish school. Didn't I hear you'd won a scholarship?"

Jonah looked directly into Cole's eyes as if willing him to understand. "Yeah, but I can't take it anymore."

"You'll graduate in four months. Then you can get out of here, go to college."

He shook his head. "I won't last that long."

He wouldn't last long on Cole's farm either, if Cole snapped and let his werewolf side take control. "Why ask me?" Cole thought he knew, but he wanted confirmation.

Jonah glanced around the restaurant. Only a few tables were occupied, and no one sat nearby. In a voice so low even Cole's sensitive ears could barely hear, he said "Cole, I'm… different, like you. If my brother finds out…"

If Nathan found out, he'd kick Jonah out, maybe beat him. Cole wished Jonah didn't stir him up so much. "I'm sorry. I've got all the hands I need right now."

The eager light went out of Jonah's eyes. He sloshed coffee on the table in his haste to get out of the booth. "OK, I understand. I'm sorry."

Cole grabbed Jonah's arm before he could run. Heat snapped between them, nearly making Cole let go. "I'm sorry for what you're going through."

Jonah shook his head. "Not sorry enough." He pulled free and left.

Jonah's condemnation hit Cole like a punch to the gut. Cole leaned back and closed his eyes, willing the thick, bitter coffee to stay down.

Chapter 1

One year later

What the hell was Cole doing at a horse rescue center? He needed some promising colts, not another stray. But he'd run into his friend April when he stopped for lunch on the way to visit a breeder, and she'd sweet-talked him into coming out to her farm to see her rescue organization's latest adoptees. Cole was probably the most soft-hearted werewolf in the history of his kind. His inability to resist a stray was legendary.

April ushered them into her kitchen and plied him with her illegally delicious chocolate chip cookies. Cole let himself relax and enjoy just sitting and talking for a while. He'd forgotten how much he enjoyed April's company. They'd met when he was in college, and when he'd moved back to Cranford, they'd gotten reacquainted, though he saw her less than he meant to. Billy, his barn manager, kept telling him to take more time off. Working all the time made Cole act old and cranky.

Eventually, they headed to the barn, and Cole braced himself for a hard sell. As they walked down the aisle looking at the latest rescues, Cole saw a quarter horse he thought a friend could use so he gave April the contact info. As they neared the end of the barn, Cole thought he was going to escape empty-handed. Then a terrified whinny broke the silence, making Cole shudder.

"That's Demon." April walked toward the heart-rending sound. "His owner died and a neighbor saved him from being destroyed and brought him here. He's been beaten and starved. He won't let any of us touch him, and he's not eating."

Cole followed her. He heard stomping and banging as if the horse was slamming himself against the stall door in his panic. His heart ached for the poor horse. "He's going to hurt himself."

April nodded. "I know. He's already been injured trying to escape. I'm scared we'll have to put him down if we can't get him to eat."

Cole reached the end of the barn and saw the roan stallion. His ribs stood out. His coat had the potential to shine like autumn leaves in the sun, but lack of grooming had made it dull, and scars and saddle sores marred his back. Demon lifted his head and stared at Cole. Suddenly the fight drained out of him.

The force of his stare made Cole step back, instincts on high alert. Something in Demon's eyes called to him, melting his heart and making the hair on the back of his neck stand up at the same time. Cole wasn't sure how he knew, but his life was about to change irrevocably.

Demon stared at Cole for several seconds, standing nearly motionless. Then he stuck his head over the door of his stall, snorted gently, and stretched his neck. He was hoping for a treat.

Cole hardly dared to breathe. Nervous horses normally got more skittish around him. He'd never been able to gentle a horse before. His human half made riding possible, but he still needed much longer to bond with a horse than a pure human would. Some of the animals grew to trust him, but the truly wild ones never accepted him.

April laid a hand on Cole's arm. "I've never seen Demon act this way. He's never shown interest in any of us."

Cole stayed where he was, but spoke to the horse in a low voice. "Easy, boy. You want a treat?"

Demon whinnied softly. Cole took a step toward him.

Demon stayed put.

Cole took a deep breath and counted to three, not wanting to move too fast. As he waited, frozen in place, he noticed something in the barn smelled familiar, a bright scent he couldn't place.

April laid a hand on his back. "Keep walking slowly. See if he stays calm."

Cole took a few more steps. Demon whinnied loudly, but it was a happy sound. No hint of his earlier terror remained. "Wait here," April instructed. She backed away slowly, and then returned with some carrots in her hand.

Cole couldn't figure out what was going on. Why would a terrified horse show an interest in him? Had a werewolf been kind to him in the past? The familiar smell tantalized him again. He tried to pull it deep enough into his lungs to figure out what it was, but memories only teased him.

Demon flared his nostrils. He smelled the carrots, but he wasn't looking at Cole's hand as most horses would. He looked right into Cole's eyes, studying him as if he knew him.

Cole had never seen this horse before. No one would forget him. If the animal hadn't been abused, he'd be stunning. But the sense that their meeting held a deep significance took hold and wouldn't let go.

Cole held out his hand, palm up, offering the carrot. Demon ate it quickly, and then nuzzled Cole's hand. Cole stared, unable to believe what he was seeing. The horse was starving. If he'd snatched the treat and backed away, Cole might have dismissed his easy acceptance of a man with wolf blood, but Demon still wanted attention. He rubbed Demon between the ears. The tantalizingly familiar smell was stronger now. Was it coming from Demon? He rubbed the horse's nose and concentrated, but he couldn't grab the memory before the scent of hay, leather, sweat, and other horses overwhelmed Cole's senses.

April cautiously stepped up beside him. "I can't believe it."

"Me either."

"He hasn't responded to anyone else. We've barely been able to take care of his wounds and offer him food without getting hurt. Then in walks a half-breed werewolf, and he's as content as can be."

"Do you think he's known a wolf before, a civilized one like me?"

April grinned. "Sweetie, there aren't many like you."

Demon snuffled as Cole scratched his ears. How could someone treat such a wonderful horse so badly? His gut knotted as he looked at the horrible scars on Demon's back. He couldn't imagine what could make someone think they needed to beat a horse. "You're going to be OK, now. You know that don't you, boy?"

Demon snorted and nodded as if truly answering. Cole smiled. "You're a smart boy, aren't you? April is going to take such good care of you."

Demon pulled back and stomped his foot as he shook his head vehemently.

Cole looked at April. "Is he saying 'no'?"

She grinned. "Looks like it." April stepped up to the door of the stall, and Demon laid his ears back. His nostrils flared. "Demon, do you want to go with Cole?"

"April." Cole growled, but Demon's ears perked up, and he nodded.

Cole didn't need another rescued animal to join the growing pack of dogs and cats, and… hell, some of his grooms were rescues too. He didn't have time for this project, but how could he say no? The last time he'd turned someone away… well… Jonah had never been found. He might have died because Cole didn't have the courage to hire him.

He couldn't atone for what he'd done to Jonah by taking in an abused horse. But ever since Jonah disappeared, Cole had been incapable of saying no to someone in need. Billy kept pointing out how expensive this habit had become. They'd nearly come to blows over his decision to hire an ex-con Cole believed had been wrongly accused. So far the man had exceeded every one of Cole's expectations.

Maybe Cole could turn Demon into an all-star horse. Demon was asking for help in the only way he could. Yes, cozying up to a man with werewolf blood was strange behavior, but Cole had already begun to think of Demon as his horse

April studied Demon carefully. "Did somebody teach you how to answer questions?"

Demon snorted and shook his head.

Cole was astounded. "Are you sure he's not a shifter?"

"If he could turn into a human, why did he stay with his former owner? Wouldn't he have shifted and run?"

Cole considered her statement. "What if he was hiding from something or someone?"

April pointed to the scars on Demon's flank. "What could make him endure that?"

Cole forced himself to look, to imagine enduring such torture. "You're right. No secret could be worth such pain."

April turned to him, but before she asked the inevitable question, he preempted her.

"Yes, I'll take him."

She grinned. "Thank you. I know Demon thanks you too."

The horse snorted and nodded vigorously.

Cole was going to nurse him back to full strength. He had horses he trusted and loved, but he'd never truly bonded with one. He could bond with Demon, he was sure of it. They were perfect for each other.

* * * *

After leaving April's, Cole spent a long, grueling day haggling with some of the best breeders in the area. Fortunately, his efforts paid off. He purchased two beautiful colts, the most perfectly gaited Tennessee walkers he'd seen since he'd taken over the farm. If his instincts were right, he'd gotten them at a bargain price.

Rain poured down on him all afternoon. He was splattered with mud, sweat-soaked after the adrenaline rush of haggling for fine horseflesh, and starving. He wanted to run into the house, grab something to eat, and take a hot shower, but he had to see to Demon first.

A terrified whinny sent Cole rushing to the trailer. "I'll lead him out."

His trainer, Danielle, eyed him as if he'd lost his mind. "I don't mean to disrespect you, Boss, but I'm not sure you're the best one to coax him out."

"I'm the only one who can coax him out."

Billy gave Danielle a look that told her to back off. She did, though she obviously wanted to know what was going on.

Cole approached the trailer. "Demon, it's OK. I'm here." He kept his voice low, talking like he would to a shy dog rather than a horse, an animal that "got" him, that could be convinced he was part of Cole's pack.

The horse calmed and Cole climbed into the trailer. He rubbed Demon's flank as he approached. "Easy, boy. We're on my farm now. I need to put a halter on you and lead you to a stall. No one here will hurt you."

Demon's eyes were wide. A shiver ran along his back, and he tossed his head.

"Shhh!" Cole leaned close and hugged Demon's neck. "I know this is hard. You've been hurt, but so have a lot of us here. We want to help you."

Demon pawed the floor of the trailer. His ears swiveled, trying to interpret all the new sounds and check for danger.

Cole sighed. He worried his legs would fold under him. He'd give anything to lie down on a soft bed, but Demon needed him.

"I'll stay with you as long as you need me, OK?"

Demon nodded. And snuffled softly.

Cole slipped the bridle over Demon's head, feeling the horse tremble under his hands. "I'll take it off once you're in the stall."

Demon nodded again. How the hell could the horse understand and answer so clearly if he wasn't a shifter? But April was right. A shifter would've changed and gotten free. Demon had probably been owned by someone who trained him for a circus. Although Cole had never heard of another horse who could answer complex questions so easily.

He clipped the lead rope to Demon's halter, clucked his tongue, and encouraged Demon to back out of the trailer. "Clear the way for us, or he's going to panic."

Billy, Danielle, and the grooms moved back, but they all stared.

"What the hell's going on, Boss?" Shep asked. The groom had worked for Cole's grandparents. He was the only employee who'd stayed on after they died. He'd witnessed first-hand how hard Cole worked to get the horses to accept him when he'd first come to the farm as a grieving teenager.

"I wish I knew. I don't understand it either," Cole said in a low voice as he emerged from the trailer. Demon nuzzled him and snuggled against his side as if he were a security blanket.

"Can he really talk?" another of the grooms asked.

Cole grinned. "His grammar's not so good, but he's got 'yes' and 'no' down."

"Hell, my grammar ain't so good either, city boy. You saying that horse is as smart as me?"

Cole laughed. When he got to the barn door, Demon pulled back and neighed nervously. "What is it, boy?"

Demon shook his head. Billy and Shep had entered the barn ahead of him. They were settling the colts he'd bought into their stalls.

He stepped back and scratched Demon between the ears. "You're going to have to get used to being around the other horses."

Demon snorted.

Cole tugged hard on the lead, but the horse scrambled backward. "Damn it." Cole was exhausted, tired, and hungry. He should've stopped for a burger on the way home. He tugged again.

Demon flattened his ears.

"Fuck." Cole kicked at the ground. "You're going in the barn. I'm not going to hurt you, but we've got to get you into a stall."

Demon still refused to budge. Cole forced himself to take a slow breath. "Is it the horses? Did you think you'd get a private barn?"

Demon shook his head.

"Then what the—oh, you don't want my men in the barn, right?"

Demon's ears came back up, and he gave a small nod.

"Billy, Shep, you got those colts settled?"

"Yes, sir," Shep answered.

"Then do me a favor and head on to the bunkhouse. I don't think Demon's going to let anyone else be in the barn."

Billy raised a brow. "That is one odd horse."

"Yeah, but I guess we got to give him his quirks after all he's been through."

"Sure, but cozying up to a wolf. Hmmph. No accounting for taste."

Cole flipped him off. "Fuck you."

"Let me shower first, Boss." Billy retorted.

"Ha. Like I'd want your bony ass." Cole laughed as he remembered how lucky he was to have a manager he could joke with.

"I'll make sure they leave some supper for you, Boss," Shep called as the two men headed out the far door of the barn.

Once the men were gone, Demon followed Cole into the barn without further protest. The light outside was beginning to fade. Cole turned on the lights over the aisles, but the stalls remained deeply shadowed.

Cole's stomach growled as they walked to one of the far stalls. He usually managed to keep his lupine instincts under control, but he'd let himself get way too hungry, and now the barn smelled like food. He wished Demon would let someone else groom him. By the time he got back to the house, he'd have to grab a steak from the fridge and eat it raw. Cole tried to live like a pure-blooded human, but sometimes the wolf inside him was damned hard to fight.

At least the others would be in the bunkhouse and wouldn't see him. A few months ago, Billy had caught him stuffing raw meat in his face like a maniac. Cole feared his friend would run, maybe even quit, but he just made a joke about working for a savage. Other than ribbing him about it occasionally in private, he'd never said anything else. But Billy's acceptance didn't keep Cole from being embarrassed about letting his animal needs control him.

How much pull would his predatory instincts have if he were a full-blooded werewolf? He couldn't imagine fighting stronger urges than those he already felt. No wonder so few werewolves were civilized enough to live among humans. He'd once longed to be a pureblood, but after a year of trying as hard as he could to shift with no success, he'd denied his wolf whenever possible and worked at being human.

Being pulled in both directions was tearing him apart. He imagined hunting prey on four legs, racing through the woods like sleek muscular vengeance. He'd sink his teeth into his prey and… no, best not to think about that. Such animalistic freedom might make it hard to become human again.

As he led Demon into the stall, he smelled the familiar scent again, a bit like fresh hay but orangey and bright and… young? What did that mean? Maybe he was going crazy.

He'd found a horse that preferred a half-werewolf to a human, and he believed the horse could answer his questions. Yep, he sounded crazy all right. Smelling strange things was just an added bonus. Thankfully, April had seen the horse answer him, or he'd be convinced he'd lost it.

Cole unhooked the lead rope but kept hold of Demon's halter. "Are you going to let me groom you? I promise to be gentle."

Demon nodded.

"Good. I'll be right back." Cole slipped out of the stall door, latched it behind him, and went to get a grooming kit. When he returned, Demon was waiting patiently for him. He selected a curry comb and started working the dust out of the horse's coat. Demon hadn't let anyone on April's farm groom him, and his hair was a mess. Tonight wasn't the time to really get him good and clean, but Cole wanted to make a start. He rubbed in firm circles, careful to avoid the freshest wounds which were still healing.

As he worked on Demon's flanks, the horse studied him curiously. His big brown eyes held confusion, fear, and longing—for safety? For a real home? Cole sympathized, and he hoped to God he could give Demon some security.

He finished with the curry comb and rubbed Demon's nose. "I'm going to brush you and clean your hooves. Then I'll get you some dinner."

Demon pushed against Cole's hand and watched him, his eyes soulful, familiar.

What? How could they be familiar? Cole stepped back. The barn spun around him, and the citrusy smell floated in the air again. What was wrong with him? He shook off the feeling that he was missing something important and grabbed the brush. He'd be OK once he got some protein in him. He'd just waited too long to eat. That would explain the swirling of his thoughts and the sloshy feeling in his stomach.

He brushed Demon quickly. The horse continued to watch him as if he was trying to figure something out or trying to memorize every inch of Cole. The constant attention unnerved Cole.

By the time he finished brushing Demon and cleaning his hooves, the horse's ears stood up and Cole would have sworn his mouth curled up in a smile. "Do you feel better, boy?"

Demon nodded vigorously.

"Good. I'm going to get you some hay, and then I'll have to get my own dinner."

Demon nodded again and nuzzled Cole.

Cole patted his nose before leaving the stall. He headed to the far end of the barn and grabbed a feeding bucket. But a few seconds later, a clattering sound made his skin prickle. Something was wrong. He dropped the bucket and ran to Demon's stall.

Demon wasn't there.

Jonah stood in the middle of the stall, pale and thin and completely naked.

Cole rubbed his eyes. He had really gone over the edge now. "J-Jonah?"

Chapter 2

The boy nodded. "I-yes. I'm Jonah. Cole?"

Cole nodded, unable to make his voice work. Soulful chocolate brown eyes. The smell of newly mown hay, orange groves, and clean young man. No wonder Demon seemed familiar.

"You were Demon." Cole said, finally able to speak.

Jonah nodded.

Cole couldn't verbalize his racing thoughts. He was shaking, sick at the thought of what Jonah had suffered, stunned, thankful. His knees threatened to give, and he grabbed the stall door to keep himself upright.

Jonah trembled. "My brother… he locked me in horse form. I forgot who I was. Forgot how… how to be h-human."

Rage, fear, and a fierce need to protect had Cole ready to rip Nathan Marks apart.

Jonah looked lost and confused.

Cole wanted to pull Jonah into his arms and take his fear away, but he was afraid to move. "Tell me what happened."

"C-can't, not now. I… need… hold me."

Cole opened his arms, and Jonah fell into them, squeezing him so tight he could barely breathe. Jonah's tears soaked Cole's shirt, and Cole buried his head against Jonah's neck, breathing deeply. Never again would he forget Jonah's scent. Never again would he let Jonah go.

Seconds later, their mouths found each other.

Cole was hungry and tired. He had no power to resist. He took the kisses he'd wanted so badly a year ago. He couldn't even remember why he shouldn't.

Jonah's mouth opened under Cole's insistent pressure. He moaned as Cole licked and sucked his bottom lip, and he tightened his arms around Cole's neck, grinding his full length against Cole.

Cole clasped Jonah's ass, molding them together. He gasped against Jonah's lips as Jonah's cock grew hard against him. He pushed his hand between them, grasping, stroking.

His wolf growled deep inside. Fierce hunger had him ready to sink his teeth into the tender flesh of Jonah's neck.

He pushed Jonah away, stepped back, and stumbled over the halter that had fallen to the ground when Jonah shifted. God help him. What was he doing? His chest tightened. He couldn't breathe. He closed his eyes, willing his hunger, sexual and predatory, under control.

A few seconds later, Jonah touched his arm. The boy shivered and Cole saw tears in his dark eyes.

"I'm sorry," Cole said. "I'm just hungry. I won't hurt you." He slid out of his coat and handed it to Jonah.

Jonah frowned as he took the coat and slipped it on. "You would never hurt me."

"But I did." Cole hated the sob in his voice. "None of this would have happened if I'd helped you."

"You didn't know what Nathan would do. Even I didn't… but you saved me yesterday."

Cole shook his head. "I saved a horse. I didn't know it was you."

Tears spilled over and slid down Jonah's cheeks. "When I saw you… I…" He took a shaky breath. "I remembered everything. I know you don't want me, but—"

Cole pressed a finger to Jonah's lips. He couldn't bear to hear any more, not when he wanted Jonah so badly it hurt. "I have cursed myself every day since you disappeared. I should have brought you here, should have… I was scared."

Jonah frowned. "Of what? I've never seen you back down from anyone."

How could Cole explain he'd been scared he couldn't keep his hands off Jonah? If he let himself have a touch, a taste, his wolfish nature might take over. "My werewolf blood makes it hard to control what I feel… I was scared I might…" Cole couldn't say anymore. What he might do was too horrible to confess out loud.

Jonah looked away. "It's OK. I won't ask to stay now. I just need you to help me get away, somewhere Nathan won't ever find me."

Cole couldn't breathe. His chest tightened, suffocating him. Of course Jonah wanted to get away as fast as he could. Why would he want to stay with the man who rejected him? If he'd had any other way to come back to his human form, he would have taken it and never seen Cole again. Why did the thought of Jonah running hurt so badly?

And why had kissing Jonah seemed so different from any other kiss? Jonah had just found himself again. He was probably just acting on instinct, on needs trapped for so long.

"I'll help you any way I can." As he said those words, he pulled Jonah to him. How the hell was he going to send Jonah away and never see him again? Now that Cole knew Jonah was alive, he wanted him more than ever.

They held each other in silence, Cole barely breathing, scared to move. Then Jonah kissed the side of his neck with a careful brush of his lips. Flames shot through Cole's body. His cock went from semi-hard to aching steel. Hunger roared through him.

His wolf clawed to get out. He wanted to shove Jonah down in the straw and drive into him, make him scream, pin him down with teeth and claws so he would never leave again.

Instead, he shoved Jonah away and scrambled to his feet. "I need… food. Can't. Wait."

Jonah stared at him. The smell of his fear only made Cole hotter.

"Please don't leave." He begged Jonah.

Jonah reached a shaky hand toward him, but Cole didn't take it.

"Need to know… you'll be here. Please!"

"Cole, are you OK?"

Cole shook his head and backed out of the stall, scared if he stayed he would either fuck Jonah or eat him.

"I'm not going to leave," Jonah said, clearly confused.

Cole slammed the stall door behind him and ran for the house.

Cole raced into the kitchen and jerked open the fridge door, making all the bottles rattle against each other. He grabbed a package of meat he'd intended to use for beef stew. Barely taking time to pull off the plastic wrap, he grabbed a chunk and swallowed it whole. He didn't stop until he'd eaten every piece. Then he stood there in front of the open fridge, staring at the empty package with blood running down his face.

He was a fucking animal. Those who weren't scared of him damn well should be. He had no business taking Jonah as a lover.

No matter how unfounded the fear, he'd spend every moment worried he would lose it, grow claws for real, and tear Jonah up. Plenty of his partners had feared the same thing. After they took their satisfaction, they couldn't get out of bed fast enough. And others... well... they craved the danger, begged him to bite them, but he couldn't. What if he accidentally killed them?

No, outside of occasional, anonymous encounters, he'd resigned himself to being alone. He had some good friends. He had the ranch. He had a purpose. That had to be enough. But for a few seconds, while he held Jonah, Cole had thought maybe he could have more. Then his canine hunger had come roaring to life, and he knew better.

Jonah was alive and safe. That should be satisfactory. While Cole searched for him, he told himself if he found Jonah safe, he wouldn't interfere in his new life. He'd been a fool to think he could just walk away. He still longed for Jonah the same way he had all those months ago. When Jonah left, Cole would feel as if someone had ripped away a part of him.

What was so different about Jonah? Why did someone so young have so much power over him? Was he a pervert for wanting a boy just on the cusp of adulthood?

Cole threw away the empty meat package, cleaned himself up and grabbed a chicken leg, cooked this time. He packed some food for Jonah and filled a water bottle.

He took the stairs to his room where he grabbed some sweatpants for Jonah and a fleece jacket for himself. He caught sight of his reflection in the mirror over the dresser. His dark brown hair was still damp with rain and sweat. He'd ignored the need for a haircut so long it now brushed his shoulders. His eyes, sometimes hazel and sometimes gray, were like cold rain that night, and he looked tired, older than he was. Good thing he wasn't trying to impress Jonah.

He stepped onto the porch, trying not to make a sound. He didn't want to have to explain his actions to any of his crew. He could hear the TV blaring through the open windows. Shep's truck was gone. He'd headed home to his wife. Cole saw a light in the apartment over the garage. Hopefully Danielle wouldn't look out her window and see him creeping back into the barn.

Cole's heart pounded as he walked toward Jonah's stall. Part of him was afraid the whole encounter with Jonah was a crazy dream. But Jonah was there still, sitting in the straw with his head in his hands and Cole's coat wrapped around him.

Jonah looked so young and vulnerable. Cole's free hand tightened into a fist when he thought about what he'd been through. He didn't know if he'd be able to stop himself from shooting Nathan through his black heart next time he saw him. Though the bastard deserved to be tortured first, a quick death was too good for him.

"I brought you some pants and something to eat." Cole frowned, looking at the angry marks on Jonah's back. Jonah pulled on the pants. They were laughably big, but he tightened the string and they stayed up. "Why don't we take the food back to the house, and I'll get something to put on your wounds," Cole suggested.

Jonah took the lunch box and water bottle. "No, I need to stay out here. I can't risk anyone seeing me. Shifting will speed the healing. They'll fade quickly now."

"Do you need a blanket?" Cole couldn't feel the cold. Jonah had started something burning inside Cole. Even a dip in an ice cold stream wouldn't cool him off. Once Jonah left, Cole doubted he'd be able to get warm no matter how many blankets he wrapped around himself.

Jonah shook his head. "I'm just need you to stay with me. Are you OK?"

Cole nodded and sank down into the straw next to Jonah. "I needed to eat and… uh… clear my head."

Jonah's mouth turned up a little. "Yeah, I guess you had a shock."

"I'm glad you're here."

Jonah looked down at the straw, his cheeks reddened. "I don't know if I can keep anything down," he said, looking toward the box of food. "I've only eaten hay for the last year."

He was thin, painfully so. Cole bet his ribs would show as prominently as Demon's had. "You've got to try. Sip on the water first. If you need me to, I can make you some soup or something. Anything to get some food in you."

Jonah smiled. "Thanks. I-I'll try." His hand shook as he tried to unscrew the cap.

Cole took the bottle back and removed it for him. Then Jonah took a tentative sip, rolling the water around in his mouth as if he weren't sure he remembered how to drink as a human.

Cole watched the muscles of his throat work as he swallowed. He wanted to trace the water's path with his tongue, to taste Jonah everywhere. But Jonah didn't need such complications. He'd been stuck in animal form for almost a year. He had to learn how to live as a human again. He deserved a lot more than a fucked up half-werewolf who was more than a decade older than him. Cole squeezed his eyes shut.

"Cole?"

His breath caught. "Yes?" He didn't open his eyes.

"I'm sorry."

"You have nothing to be sorry for."

"You didn't want me here, and now you're out here taking care of me when you're obviously exhausted. I would tell you to go to bed, but I don't want to be alone."

Cole's chest ached. "I'll stay as long as you need me. And I do want you here. I always did." *I just hope to God I can control myself.*

"Cole…"

Something tightened inside Cole. He could not let Jonah go. He might split apart if he did. Tears stung the backs of his eyes, but he would not fucking cry. He would hold himself together. Jonah deserved that. "You can say anything to me. I'm here for you now."

Jonah shook his head and took another sip of water. "Nothing. I should try to eat something."

Cole picked up the lunch box from where Jonah had laid it in the straw. When Jonah took it from him, their hands brushed. Cole jumped as a spark raced through him, lighting him up.

Jonah's eyes widened.

Had he felt it too?

As if in response, Jonah's tongue slid across his lower lip. Cole wanted to follow it with his own.

Jonah didn't look at him again. He unzipped the container and pulled out a chicken breast. He bit into it and chewed slowly. After the first bite, he ate faster and faster.

Cole couldn't stop staring. How could eating chicken be so damn sexy? "You OK?"

Jonah blushed. "Sorry. It's just so damn good"

Cole grinned. "Shep's wife made it. She's a genius in the kitchen."

Jonah finished the chicken and pulled out a pudding cup and a spoon. He looked up at Cole and raised his brows.

Heat flared in Cole's cheeks. "What? I like pudding."

Jonah grinned. "Me too."

Jonah's obvious happiness gave Cole a strange feeling in his chest. He watched as Jonah pulled the foil off the top of the container and dug in with his spoon. He looked as if he was trying to resist gobbling it down. If Jonah did stay on the ranch, Cole would have him filled out in no time.

If? What the fuck was he thinking? Jonah couldn't stay. Cole had to accept it.

Jonah finished the pudding, put the spoon down, and licked his lips. He looked at the container as if he wasn't sure what to do with it. Cole reached for it as Jonah's tongue swiped the last of the pudding from his lip. Cole shuddered.

He stood, knowing he shouldn't be so close to Jonah. But Jonah stood too,. Now he was so near, they almost touched.

Chapter 3

"Cole?"

Cole swallowed, trying to make his voice work. "What?"

"Kiss me."

Cole's body screamed for him to taste Jonah, just one more time. He forced himself to move farther away from the temptation of Jonah's full lips. He shook his head. "Can't."

Jonah closed his eyes and took a deep breath. "I've wanted you for so long. When you wouldn't hire me, I decided I could make it to graduation like you said. Then I was going to come out here and demand you give me a chance to work for you. When Nathan locked me in animal form, I thought I'd never see you again. And then I forgot everything. But now I remember. I remember just how much I need you. Please. Just one more time before I leave."

Cole wanted him so bad it hurt. "You make me wild, crazy. I'm afraid I might hurt you."

Jonah shook his head. "Your wolf senses my stallion. He wants to run, but he wants your wolf to chase him, to catch him, to take him down and—"

Cole dropped the pudding container onto the floor, took Jonah's face in his hands, and kissed him. There was nothing gentle about it this time.

Passion poured out of him into Jonah, and Jonah met every fierce thrust of his tongue.

Jonah pulled Cole's shirt from his jeans and slid his hands up Cole's back. The heat from Jonah's hands made Cole groan into his mouth as he sucked on his tongue, drawing whimpers from him.

Cole released Jonah's lips and kissed his neck, breathing in the scent that tantalized him when Jonah was in horse form. He nipped and licked, and Jonah ground against him, clinging to him desperately.

Cole sank to his knees and undid Jonah's sweats. The fabric slid easily from his slight hips. Cole wrapped a hand around Jonah's cock which was thick and fleshy and fucking perfect. His body might not look like a stallion's right now, but his cock sure as hell did. He nuzzled Jonah's stomach and kissed the smooth skin as he skimmed a hand through the narrow line of hair that widened just above base of his cock.

"Let me help you. Let me heal you," he whispered against Jonah's soft skin.

Jonah shivered. "Please."

Cole was putting Jonah in danger, taking something he didn't deserve to have, but he couldn't stop himself. He kissed the tip of Jonah's cock before taking it into his mouth.

Jonah moaned. "Yes, oh, yes."

Cole sucked, loving the feel of Jonah's thick, hard flesh in his mouth. He tried to swallow all of him, but Jonah was too big. He pulled back and licked the head.

Jonah fisted his hand in Cole's hair. "Please."

Cole took Jonah's shaft back in his mouth and clasped his hips, steadying himself. He sucked hard, sliding up and down Jonah's shaft.

Jonah made small thrusts with his hips. Cole could feel the tension in him. He pulled back and looked up at Jonah. "Fuck my mouth. Use me."

"Cole!"

"Do it." Cole growled.

Cole took him deep and pulled his ass cheeks apart, letting his fingers skim over Jonah's hole, teasing him. "Fuck!" Jonah shouted as he thrust hard into Cole's mouth, making him choke.

"Sorry," Jonah said and tried to pull away, but Cole held him tight.

Cole licked and nipped at the underside of Jonah's cock before saying anything. "No apologies."

"But—"

Cole looked up at Jonah, licked the very tip of his cock. "Take what you want."

Jonah made a strangled cry and drove in. Cole groaned around the hardness and relaxed his mouth so he could take whatever Jonah needed to give.

Jonah's thrusts grew faster, frantic. Cole took all of him, needing to please Jonah, to make him happy, to taste his pleasure.

"Cole, I'm going to—" He tried to pull out, but Cole squeezed his ass, trapping him, and he cried out. Hot jets of cum poured down Cole's throat. Jonah's orgasm seemed to go on forever, but Cole swallowed every drop of his salty seed.

Cole let Jonah's softening shaft slide from his mouth, placing gentle kisses along the length before he sat back on his knees.

Jonah looked at him, eyes dark. "I-I've never. Wow!" His knees gave out, and Cole caught him as he crashed to the straw.

Cole stretched out alongside him, and Jonah reached for him. Jonah wrestled with the opening of Cole's jeans until he could wrap a hand around Cole's shaft.

Cole sucked in his breath. "I'm close. You taste so damn good."

"Really?"

Cole leaned over and kissed him. Jonah lapped at his mouth, groaning, cock hardening again. Damn, did all shifters have amazing recovery? His mind spun fantasies of fucking Jonah over and over all night.

He pulled back, suddenly determined Jonah should stay. He wanted to take him inside, to a bed where they'd be more comfortable. To hell with what he *should* do. He couldn't let this boy go. Jonah was his. He'd learn control. He'd find a way.

Jonah licked his lips and tightened his hold on Cole's cock before giving him long firm strokes. "I want to suck you, but I've never…"

Cole groaned. The idea of being Jonah's first made him crazy. "You've never sucked a man?"

"Never been with a man at all." His cheeks turned bright red.

Cole thought he might die right there. Jonah was a virgin. The idea terrified him and excited him so much he thought his skin might split. No other man had touched Jonah, slid into him, had his hot mouth around his cock.

Cole wanted to be his first. He wanted to be the only one to take Jonah. He growled. His wolf's protectiveness flared into action. Jonah was his. Instincts warred inside him, possessiveness and hunger. His wolf loved the idea of tearing into Jonah's vulnerable virgin body, of taking, owning, but Cole would hold him back. He could be gentle when he needed to.

"Tell me if I'm not doing this right." Jonah lowered his head into Cole's lap and took Cole's cock into his mouth.

Cole fought his urge to thrust into the wet heat. "Feels so good."

Jonah smiled around him and sucked. Cole wasn't going to last more than a few seconds. Jonah's mouth felt like heaven. Cole would never have known this was his first blow job. Jonah instinctively knew exactly what Cole wanted.

Cole realized his hands were grasping Jonah's head, guiding him farther onto his cock. He tried to stop, but he couldn't.

Jonah stretched out on his stomach in the straw so he could get the best possible access to Cole's cock. He licked and sucked, and Cole fought his instincts. His wolf growled and panted, wanting him to flip Jonah over and drive into him, grind him into the straw, stuff his ass until he screamed.

Cole didn't dare touch Jonah now. He dug his fingers into his thighs. Fire slid from his toes up his body as lighting struck his spine and sped downward. "Fuck, Jonah. I'm coming I can't—" He shot into Jonah's mouth. He'd meant to warn him sooner, but Jonah stole his ability to think.

Jonah sputtered at the force of Cole's orgasm. He pulled back, but he guided Cole's second shot into his open mouth. The sight made Cole convulse. Jonah pumped his cock, taking every drop he had to give.

When he was done, Jonah grinned. "Wow. That was… I wish…"

"I want to fuck you." The words tumbled out of Cole's mouth before he could stop them. He was the big bad wolf stalking innocent prey. His cock hadn't even softened. The sight of Jonah happily swallowing his cum did something insane to him.

Jonah smiled. "I want you to be my first. But I'm…"

Cole stroked his face. "I'll be gentle. I know I'm not… I like it rough, but I can be easy with you." *Please, let me be telling the truth.*

"I trust you."

He shouldn't. Cole had come back to the barn convinced he had to send Jonah away, to keep his hands off at all costs. But the feel of Jonah's lips around his cock convinced him there was no way in hell Jonah was going anywhere. Some objective part of him realized letting himself be swayed by the fact he'd survived a blow job without ripping Jonah apart wasn't right. He might lose control once he got inside Jonah, but he couldn't stop.

There were so many things Cole wanted to say. He wanted to beg Jonah not to go, to tell him he would avenge his torture, care for him, heal him. But if he started talking, he would babble, growl, and probably scare the shit out of Jonah, so he simply said, "Let's go inside."

The color drained from Jonah's face. "Someone might see me. I can't let anyone know I'm here. I can't—"

"It's OK. We'll stay here." Cole's bed would be much more comfortable, but Jonah was still a skittish horse. If Cole pushed him for more than the pleasure they were sharing, he might run. Cole couldn't handle that, not now they'd gone this far. *Please let me stay in control!*

"Let me get a blanket." He practically ran to the tack room and grabbed one of the old blankets from a shelf. He hurried back and spread it on the floor of the stall. "This will feel better."

Cole quickly shucked his clothes, and Jonah tossed Cole's coat to the ground and stretched out on the blanket. Cole could smell his fear, but Jonah's cock was hard and wanting. He stroked it absently as he watched Cole.

Cole stared at Jonah's hand, licking his lips as he watched Jonah's fingers barely circling his own girth. Cole almost never bottomed, but the thought of that thick flesh driving inside him made him feel unhinged. He would get Jonah to fuck him one day, *if* Jonah stayed.

Cole sucked two fingers, coating them with saliva, wishing they were in the house where he had lube, especially for Jonah's first time, but he wouldn't risk leaving Jonah long enough to get it. At least he didn't have to worry about condoms since Jonah was a shifter and immune to human STDs.

He dropped to his knees and settled between Jonah's bent legs. He slipped his hand between Jonah's ass cheeks, still watching the slow progress of Jonah's hand up and down his shaft. He teased Jonah's tight pucker for a few seconds. "I don't want to hurt you."

"Don't care. Just need you."

Cole bit his lip to hold in a groan.

"I've… uh… used my fingers and… other things… I've just never been with anyone else." Jonah looked away, embarrassed.

The thought of Jonah fucking himself made Cole crazy. He fully intended to watch sometime. He pushed a digit inside Jonah's warmth and gasped as Jonah's ass squeezed him. He pushed in more, and Jonah groaned. "Fuck, that's good."

Cole smiled. "That's nothing. I'm going to drive you insane." He added a second finger, and Jonah made a choked sound. "You OK?'

Jonah stared at him, eyes wide, mouth open. "I think so."

He pushed in a little more.

Jonah closed his eyes. "It burns but it's good."

Cole grinned. "It's going to get even better." He worked his fingers deeper, seeking Jonah's sweet spot. He curled them forward as he slid slowly out.

Jonah's body jerked. "Oh, God!" he cried out.

Cole laughed. "Feel good?"

"Do it again."

He did. Jonah squirmed under him, fucking himself on Cole's fingers. "More." He gasped.

"You want this?" Cole stroked his cock with his other hand.

Jonah watched him. Cole's cock wasn't as big as Jonah's, but it wasn't small either.

Slowly, Jonah nodded.

"I'm going to go as slow as I can."

"OK. Just—"

"What?"

Jonah laughed. "Hurry!"

Cole smiled. Warmth that was more than sex raced through his body. He spit on his fingers and worked more moisture into Jonah's ass.

Jonah sat up. "Let me help." Cole shifted position so Jonah could suck his cock. After a few minutes, Cole pulled back, shaking with need. He loved seeing his cock sloppy with Jonah's spit.

Jonah lay back and pulled up his legs as Cole guided his cock to Jonah's hole. Cole watched as the tip of his cock disappeared into his lover.

He pushed forward, and Jonah stretched around him. He was so fucking tight.

"Are you OK?"

"Don't stop!"

Cole pushed deeper, and his cockhead popped through the thick ring of muscle.

Jonah whimpered.

Cole froze. Sweat dripped down his face. His wolf snarled, wanting freedom. He would have sworn claws were sliding out of his fingers. "Jonah!"

Jonah squeezed his eyes shut and panted. "I'm fine. It… it hurts, but I want more." He pushed back against Cole, forcing Cole deeper.

Cole growled. "Don't move."

Jonah thrust his hips. "Fuck me."

Cole pushed in all the way. His balls slapped against Jonah's ass. Jonah cried out, "Holy fuck!"

Cole squeezed Jonah's thighs, fighting the urge to pull back and slam in again. He'd gone too hard and too fast.

Jonah squirmed under him, but Cole lay over Jonah, trapping his legs between them. "Give me a sec. Don't want to hurt you."

Jonah snarled. "I won't fucking break."

Jonah's scent intoxicated Cole. He wanted to scratch, to bite, to fuck until Jonah screamed. "I can't do this."

"You *are* doing it."

Cole kept his eyes shut, not wanting to see hurt in Jonah's eyes. "We have to stop."

"No stopping. You're going to ride my ass until I blow my load all over myself."

"Baby." Who the hell taught him to talk like that?

"I want the wolf inside you."

Cole pulled out and pushed back in hard. Something broke inside him, and he drove in over and over.

Jonah cried out under him, but he arched up for more. His fingers dug into Cole's upper arms, and he murmured Cole's name over and over.

Cole licked his neck, tasting the vulnerable flesh. His wolf screamed for him to bite. He pulled out and slapped Jonah's ass. "Turn over. Now."

Jonah scrambled to obey, flipping over and positioning himself on hands and knees. Cole thrust back in, pushing Jonah down onto the blanket. He wrapped an arm around Jonah's waist and jerked him back, driving deep. He grabbed a handful of Jonah's hair with the other hand, holding him still so he could sink his teeth into the back of Jonah's neck.

"Yes! Bite me!"

Cole held him as he pounded deep. Jonah screamed, and Cole hoped it was a shout of pleasure. There was no way in hell he could stop.

Jonah stroked his own cock as he shoved his hips back to meet Cole's. "I'm so close. I'm—"

Jonah shuddered, and his ass squeezed Cole's cock, dragging Cole over too. He shoved into his lover in short harsh strokes as he spilled in his ass. He let go of Jonah's neck and lapped at the wound before collapsing on top of him.

Chapter 4

Long moments passed before either of them moved. When Jonah wiggled underneath him, Cole rolled over onto his back and pulled Jonah into the crook of his arm. Jonah lapped at Cole's sweaty chest before snuggling in and throwing a leg over him.

Cole enjoyed being still with him after the storm of need played itself out. But before too long he noticed the hay poking him through the blanket and the hardness of the concrete floor. "We should clean up."

Jonah tensed. "I need to stay here."

"We both need a shower, and we'd be a lot more comfortable in a soft bed."

Jonah shook his head. "No one can know I'm here."

Cole's gut twisted. He'd assumed Jonah wouldn't be able to walk away after what they'd shared. No matter how wrong it was or how dangerous, he couldn't send Jonah on his way now. He'd never connected with anyone the way he just had with Jonah. "You still want to leave." It wasn't a question.

Jonah nodded against his chest. "I have to."

"I won't let anyone hurt you."

"Nathan will come after you."

"I'll fucking kill him." Cole meant it, too. If Nathan tried to hurt Jonah again, Cole would put him down.

"No one can know I was here. That's safest for both of us."

Safe. The hell with safe. Cole had blown his chance to take the safe path when he'd taken Jonah's hard cock into his mouth. "My crew will know Demon's gone. They're going to want to know how and why."

Jonah shuddered. "I'll change back. You can put me out in a pasture, and I'll escape."

He pulled away from Cole and sat up, backing to the other side of the stall. He tensed and closed his eyes. *Fuck! He's going to shift.* Cole scrambled to his feet. "Don't. Please don't. I can protect you."

Jonah's body convulsed, but he didn't change. He bent over and retched.

Cole held him until the awful spasms stopped. Then he pulled Jonah into his arms, holding him tightly as he shivered violently. Cole picked up his coat from the floor and wrapped it around him.

"I'm t-too scared."

Cole stroked his scarred back "You don't ever have to be Demon again unless you want to."

"I need to leave, but what if I change and I can't figure out how to be human again?"

Cole tightened his hold on Jonah. "You don't have to leave. Your brother needs to pay for what he's done. If you stay, I'll make sure he does."

Jonah shook his head against Cole's shoulder. "He'll win. He always does."

"Does your mother know? She might help us."

Jonah pulled back. Tears streaked his face. "She let him have me."

"She knew?" Cole's gut twisted. How could she do such a thing?

"She might think he just sent me away. I don't know. She loves me, I think. In her own way. But ever since my dad left, she's never been the same."

Cole needed to keep Jonah there, keep him talking. He sank down on the blanket, pulling Jonah onto his lap. "Tell me what happened."

Jonah was silent for several long seconds then he started to speak in a low voice. "My dad got real sick when I was six. The doctors didn't think he'd make it. Some of Mama's friends came and prayed for him. When he got better, she believed their prayers had healed him. She started going to their church, and she got more and more conservative. She started telling us becoming horses was sinful and quoting the Bible at us every time she turned around. Daddy loved her, but he couldn't take it. He was happy with who he was, and he needed his freedom, so he took off.

"Mama was heartbroken. She lost her spark. Then Preacher Ted took over the church, and things got worse. She'd always been hard on me, but I knew she loved me. After she married him, she started treating me like Nathan does, like I'm not worth shit." Jonah's voice broke. He buried his face against his knees and sobbed.

Cole wanted to help. He would do anything to take this hell away from Jonah.

Jonah looked up at him. "How, Cole? How could they do this?"

Cole stared down at him helplessly. "I don't know. But I'm here. It's going to be OK."

"I can't stay here."

Panic seized Cole. He needed Jonah in a way that scared him. "How can you walk away after what we just did?"

"I can't risk staying here."

Jonah might as well have slapped him. Pain tightened his chest then anger roared through him. At Jonah. At himself. At Nathan Marks who'd dared to hurt this beautiful young man. Cole grabbed his pants and shoved his legs in hard enough to rip the fabric.

Jonah stood and took hold of Cole's arm, but Cole shook him off and fastened his pants. He looked around the stall frantically. Where was his shirt? He needed to get out of there before the hot tears stinging the back of his eyes started to spill.

"Cole, look at me."

He looked everywhere but at Jonah. If he saw those gorgeous eyes, full of pity for him, he wasn't going to be able to hold it together. "I deserve this. I deserve to find you and lose you again. To be the one who gets left this time."

"No, you deserve to run your farm without fighting a battle against my family and most of the town."

"They already talk about me. I'm a gay, half-breed werewolf horse trainer. Hell, I'd talk about me too. I don't give a damn about any of it."

"You would care when they started saying how you corrupted an innocent boy. Nasty looks are one thing. Nathan would have them out for blood."

Cole froze. He clenched his fists in his shirt, stretching the fabric. "Corrupting you? Is that what—"

"My brother found some pictures."

Cole turned then and looked at Jonah. His face and chest were flushed red, and he wouldn't meet Cole's eyes. "Porn?"

"Not exactly."

Anger seared through Cole. "He did this to you because of some pictures that weren't exactly porn?"

"Yeah. I mean he already wanted to get rid of me, but the pictures pushed him over the edge, because…"

Cole took Jonah's hands in his. All his anger focused on Jonah's family now. He would take care of Jonah. He would convince him to stay, but right now, he would just listen. "You can tell me anything."

"The pictures were of you."

Heat curled in Cole's belly. Jonah had kept pictures of him. Maybe jerked off thinking of him.

"I took them at the fair when you were showing Firestar. You had on really tight faded jeans and that green shirt that makes your eyes look greener than usual and…" Jonah blushed even darker. "I hope you don't mind."

Cole grinned. "Trust me. I don't mind at all." He wanted Jonah again right then and there.

But the wistful smile faded from Jonah's face. "Nathan said you should be taken care of. That men like you shouldn't be allowed in a decent town. I told him you were a better man than he'd ever be."

Cole winced. "What happened then?" He hated to make Jonah talk about the hell he'd been through, but he needed to know, and Jonah needed to tell someone who cared about him before he started talking to the sheriff.

"He hit me. Knocked me out. Things are fuzzy from there. I remember him telling me he was going to send me away, make me live like an animal since I was no better than one. He dragged me to the barn. I tried to fight, but my head was swimming. Maybe he'd already drugged me, or maybe his fist rattled my brain. He gave me a shot of something, and I started to change form. I couldn't stop it."

Rage burned in Cole's gut. How could Nathan do that to his own brother? "He probably used Zenethldrine"

"What's that?"

"An illegal shifter drug. It forces you into animal shape and locks you there for a day or two, more if you're given an overdose."

Jonah nodded. "I couldn't change back. I remember trying, being terrified. I couldn't find my human form. The change had always been easy for me. I fought Nathan and his friends, but I couldn't get loose."

"What friends? Who helped him do this to you?"

"Bruce Landry. Tom Wilmet. Maybe some others, but I remember seeing the two of them. They were always with Nathan, did whatever he said."

"They're going to pay. All of them. You're going to stay and tell your story to Sheriff Trent, and we're going to fight this."

Jonah rubbed Cole's arm like Cole was the one who needed comforting. "Nathan won't let us win. He's got too many supporters, and none of them are going to stand for him having an openly gay brother living right here in town."

"Nathan and his friends won't have to stand it. They'll be in prison."

Jonah shook his head. "Nathan always wins."

"I'll bring in lawyers from as far away as I need to. I'll do whatever I have to. He will pay."

Jonah's eyes looked profoundly sad. "It won't work. I need to leave now before I end up hurting you."

"You're not going to hurt me unless you leave."

Jonah looked down at the ground. "I can't—"

Maybe talking about what happened would make him angry enough to stay and fight. "Tell me what happened after he drugged you."

"He sold me to a horse breeder, one who doesn't care where his horses go as long as he makes plenty of money, one who wouldn't tell where I came from. The breeder sold me to a circus. The conditions were terrible. I kept trying to change. And then—I don't know—I guess I went crazy, because I couldn't think like a human anymore.

"I remember telling myself I'd never been human. I was a horse. But I still wouldn't do the tricks they tried to teach me. They sold me to Biggs. He beat me until I did what he said. By then, I'd forgotten everything. All I remember now is pain, hunger, fear, and knowing something wasn't right."

Cole thought he might vomit. He wasn't sure he would have survived being forced to change form, to stay an animal, or being beaten until he couldn't fight back, and slowly losing his humanity. "We have to confront this or you're always going to be running. You'll never be free until Nathan is brought to justice."

"We?" Jonah's eyes were wide.

"I would never let you fight this alone. I… fuck, this sounds so barbaric, but—" He took a long deep breath, pulling Jonah's scent into him. "My wolf sees you as mine, and as alpha here, it's my duty to protect you."

Color infused Jonah's cheeks. "I want to be yours, but I don't want to bring you pain."

"This is my choice. You're not bringing it to me, I'm taking it on."

"I want to stay here. I want to have a place to run free, to embrace my horse form again rather than seeing it as torture, but I'm scared."

Cole brushed a lock of hair off Jonah's forehead. "I want all that for you too, and I will help you have it."

"I used to love my horse form. When I ran on four legs, I was free. As a human I was caged in, like I wasn't who I was meant to be."

"Your family wanted you to be someone else, but you are exactly who you were meant to be— human and horse. Never let anyone tell you otherwise. I could've stayed away from this place, bought another spread or stayed in the city, pretended I wasn't a wolf, pretended I was straight, but I'm not going to live like that. I'm a Wilder. This is my farm, and I'm not giving it up. Nor will I give up my right to love anyone I choose."

"When he finds out I'm here, my brother will sink his teeth in and not let go."

Cole grinned. "That's OK. I may not have fangs in truth, but I can put up a hell of a fight."

Jonah laid his hands on Cole's shoulders, his expression serious. "You'll need fangs and guns too."

Cole laid his hands on top of Jonah's. "I will defend you no matter how far this goes."

"Thank you. No one's ever cared like that."

"Well, I do."

Jonah smiled.

Cole noticed they were both shivering. The night had grown considerably colder since he'd come back to the barn. "Come inside with me. We'll gather my men in the morning and tell them what's up. I'll give them a chance to leave if they want, before things get tough. Then, we'll call the sheriff."

Jonah hesitated, chewing his lower lip.

"Once we've dealt with Nathan, I won't try to stop you if you still want to leave, if the memories are too bad, or you just need more than you can have in Cranford." Cole's heart ached as he said those words, but he couldn't claim to be fighting for Jonah's freedom then trap him there.

"Wh-what if I don't want to go?"

Cole smiled. "Then you have a home here."

Jonah shivered. "I'm scared."

"So am I, but I won't let it stop me."

Jonah squeezed Cole's hands. "Me either."

Cole kissed him gently. "Get dressed. We've got to be up at dawn."

Jonah pulled on the sweatpants Cole had brought him. "I haven't worn clothes in over a year or slept in a bed. I don't feel like this is real. I'm…"

His hands shook so badly he could barely get the pants pulled up. Cole picked up his T-shirt and helped Jonah put it on before wrapping his coat back around him. "It's real. I'm real. No dream could ever be as good as what we shared."

Jonah grinned. "Yeah, no dream could make my ass this sore either."

"Fuck, Jonah, I'm sorry."

He grinned. "I kinda like it."

Oh, shit, he shouldn't say things like that. Cole was hard again. He had to reach down and adjust himself inside his jeans. He thought about pinning Jonah against the wall, lifting him and driving deep. His wolf didn't care if it hurt. He wanted to take Jonah again and again until he couldn't possibly deny Cole's claim on him.

"Cole?" Jonah trembled.

Cole smelled fear and lust, a heady combination for a wolf.

He forced himself to turn away and open the stall door. "We should get in the house. It's getting cold and—"

"What?" There was a teasing note in his voice.

"If we don't, I'm going to shove you against the wall and take you again."

Jonah exhaled a shaky breath. "I wouldn't mind that, but a bed might be nice."

Cole turned to face him again, leaning against the stall door. "I fantasized about you too, you know. Before you disappeared. Before you asked me to hire you. That's partly why I turned you down. You were so young, and I wanted you so badly."

"Wasn't it obvious I wanted you back? I don't think I was very subtle."

Cole grinned. "You weren't, but I didn't think I could restrain myself with you. And I didn't think I had any business fucking an eighteen-year-old. I wanted you to have a chance to meet someone your own age, to pursue a life outside Cranford if you wanted to."

"But you've changed your mind?" Jonah looked hopeful.

Cole nodded. "I realized I can't fight what I feel for you. Even though I'm struggling to control my werewolf side around you, even though you're still too damn young. I want you. After you disappeared, I hated myself for being afraid of what I felt for you. I tried to convince myself you didn't really want me, that you just had a crush on me because I was safe. But I couldn't stop thinking about you. I would have asked you out after you graduated, but you disappeared."

"I would have said 'yes.' I wanted you more than anything. I realized I liked men when I was about fourteen, the first time I saw you. What I came to understand was I can look at other men and think they're hot, but none of them affect me like you do."

"My wolf sees you as prey. I'm scared of what might happen, scared I will hurt you."

"You didn't hurt me tonight. Even when I felt the wolf rise inside you. My stallion screamed for me to run, but I knew you wouldn't hurt me."

Cole couldn't be so sure. "I've never shifted before, but my wolf feels so real."

"He is real, but you don't have to fear him. When a shifter changes, his animal instincts are stronger, but his human brain is still in control."

"Then why do so many werewolves attack humans?"

"They choose to ignore the warnings of their human side and enjoy the rush of power their wolf can give them. So do lots of other shifters, but they don't have to."

Cole frowned, still not convinced. "I tried to hold myself back tonight. But then you asked me to kiss you, and I couldn't deny myself anymore."

"I couldn't leave without tasting you."

Cole grinned. "Once I tasted you, I couldn't let you leave."

"Are you really sure you want me here?"

"Yes." Cole was more than willing to confront Nathan and his friends and make them pay for what they'd done to Jonah. What scared him more was facing his inner wolf and learning to balance both sides of himself without losing control. But he would do anything to keep Jonah with him.

This wouldn't be an easy path for Jonah either. Cole was asking him to face his demons, to rehash his torment, to confront his family, a family who'd rather he be dead than gay. "Are *you* sure?"

Jonah took a long, slow breath. "If I get to stay with you, then it's worth the fight."

"You can stay with me as long as you like."

"I don't know if I can face Nathan. I want to be with you, but I wish I could just forget everything that's happened to me."

"If you run now, you'll have to keep on running."

Jonah nodded. "You're going to have to help me. To hold me when I want to run."

Cole pulled Jonah into his arms. "Always."

Chapter 5

The alarm clock blared. Cole flopped his arm out, slapping at it, trying to find the snooze. He'd been having such a good dream. Warm legs tangled with his. A soft, long-fingered hand circled his cock. Fingers combed through the hair on his chest.

Why was it so fucking dark? He blinked and forced his eyes to focus on the clock. Why had he set it for five o'clock?

Then the hand from the dream slid slowly up and down his cock, and the warm legs rubbed along his own. "Cole?"

That voice, that low husky whisper. Jonah. How many nights had he dreamed of Jonah?

The grip on his cock tightened. Fingers brushed one of his nipples. He groaned. This wasn't a dream. "Want you, Cole."

He opened his eyes again. Jonah lay next to him. He could just make out his grin in the light from the clock and the moon.

He hadn't dreamed it. Jonah was here. He reached out, slid his hand into Jonah's hair, and pulled them together. Their lips met, and Cole gasped at the explosion of raw need. He could taste it, hot and sharp on Jonah's tongue. How could he trust Cole enough for this? Cole didn't deserve it, but he couldn't stop himself from taking what Jonah offered.

Jonah let go of his cock, and they wrapped their arms around each other, mouths never pulling apart. Jonah hooked his leg over Cole, squeezing their bodies together. Cole rolled, pulling Jonah up and over on him.

Jonah sucked Cole's bottom lip as he slid his hands up and down Cole's chest. "I love the feel of you, hairy and strong, just like a wolf. I want to lick you everywhere."

Cole groaned. "Anything. Do anything to me."

Jonah nipped at Cole's neck, his collar bone. He pushed Cole's arms up and buried his head in Cole's arm pit, licking, kissing, sucking the hair there. Then he concentrated on Cole's nipples, sucking one while pinching the other. All the time, he flexed his hips, rubbing their cocks together. Sensation beat at Cole, overwhelming him, but he didn't want any of it to stop.

Bang! The screen door slammed shut. Footsteps clomped into the kitchen. "Cole, you up?"

Jonah scrambled off him, and Cole sat up, swinging his legs off the side of the bed. "Be right there, Billy."

He jumped up, yanked open a drawer, and pulled out some boxers. "You stay here," he whispered to Jonah as he pulled them on. "I'm going to get some coffee going and gather the men so we can tell your story to everyone at once, OK?"

"OK." Jonah's response was almost a whisper. He looked pale, scared, and really young. Fuck. Not the way Cole wanted this day to start. *Please God, don't let Jonah change his mind and run.*

He rushed to kitchen as he pulled on some sweats. "What the hell are you doing here this early?"

Billy ran a hand through his hair. "Demon's gone! I couldn't sleep so I thought I'd go check on the new horses. He's not in his stall. I can't see him in any of the near pastures, not that you can see much of anything this early, but I—"

Cole held up his hand. "I know where he is."

"You moved him? Why?"

"Yes and no. It's a long story. Just take my word for it. He's safe."

"What the hell is going on? Something was strange with that horse from the get-go." Billy looked hurt. They usually told each other everything.

"He's a shifter. That's not the whole story, but I promise if I can get some coffee and breakfast I'll tell you the rest. Give me an hour, gather everyone, and I'll tell you all at once."

"A shifter? Why did he stay in animal form?"

"Please, Billy. Let me tell this my way."

Tense silence hung in the kitchen. Finally, Billy sighed. "I've never had a reason not to trust you. I just… well, I guess you'd say my hackles are up. Feels like a storm's brewing."

Billy was so damn perceptive. He was wise in ways you wouldn't expect from a man who billed himself as nothing more than your average hick cowboy, well, an average hick cowboy that liked men. But unlike Cole, he hadn't let the world in on his preferences, not after his family's reaction.

"You could say that. I hope you'll be willing to see it through."

Billy nodded. "We've been through a lot together. But something's got me spooked."

Billy filled his mug with "the good coffee". He'd been sneaking over here to the house in the mornings since he discovered the true depths of Cole's coffee snobbery. Now he was almost as spoiled as Cole. Cup full, he left without another word. The door banged behind him, echoing loudly.

Cole scrambled eggs, fried up bacon, and popped some bread in the toaster. When everything was ready, he made two plates and placed them on a tray with two cups of coffee.

When he opened the door to his bedroom, Jonah sat up in bed, eyes wide. "That smells amazing. No one's ever brought me breakfast in bed before."

"I've never brought anyone breakfast in bed. Actually, I've never had anyone spend the night." Yet having Jonah there was the most natural thing in the world.

"Really, you've never brought a man back here?"

Cole shook his head. "Never trusted anyone enough." But Jonah was special. Already a part of him. *How can I be sure so fast?*

He set the tray down between them on the bed. "I told Billy to gather everyone in the bunkhouse in an hour."

Jonah paled. "I don't know if I can—"

"You don't have to say anything if you don't want to. I'll tell them what they need to know."

"You shouldn't have to. It's my story."

"I told you I'm here to take care of you."

"I—"

Cole stroked Jonah's cheek with the back of his hand. "You deserve to be cared for. You deserve to be loved."

"But, you don't have to—"

"I want to."

Jonah nodded. He wrapped shaky hands around his coffee cup. Cole was determined to make a home for Jonah, a place he didn't have to be frightened. Nothing was worth fighting for more than that.

* * * *

Cole and Jonah stepped onto the porch. Billy, Danielle, Shep and the others were gathered around the picnic table at the side of the bunkhouse. Cole took a deep breath. He reached for Jonah's hand. Jonah gave him a surprised look. "I want this in the open. If they have a problem, they can leave."

Jonah squeezed Cole's hand. They walked toward Cole's crew. Some were standing, some were sitting, but they all turned and stared. A few looked scared as hell. Most of them recognized Jonah, but even those who didn't sensed something serious was going down.

Billy pushed away from the tree he'd been leaning against. He looked ready to say something, but Cole held up his hand. "For those of you that don't know, this is Jonah Marks."

"Agnes Marks' son? The one who went missing?" Danielle asked.

Cole and Jonah both nodded. "Over a year ago, Jonah's brother, Nathan, found out Jonah was gay. Nathan and some friends forced Jonah into his horse form and sold him to a black market breeder. The torment caused Jonah to lose the ability to shift back. I found him at April's Haven, having been beaten and starved by his previous 'owner'. "

"Did you know?" Billy asked looking like he was working up quite a head of steam.

"No. I wondered if he was a shifter, but neither April or I thought a shifter would've endured that kind of starvation and torture. And then—"

Jonah squeezed his hand. "Then I remembered who I was. Seeing Cole. Recognizing him and listening to his voice brought my human side back. I remembered everything that happened, and the ability to change returned."

"What happens now?" Billy asked. He still looked pissed.

"We call the sheriff. Jonah needed comfort last night, not a bunch of questions. I took care of him, but now it's time to take action."

One of the men gave a low whistle. Cole glared at him. Several of the others laughed, and Jonah's cheeks flushed pink.

Billy just looked at Cole, eyes uncertain. "Were you… together before? I thought—"

"No. Jonah wanted to work for me before he was abducted. I turned him down. He was too young, and I wanted him too much."

Cole looked around, all eyes were on him. He had to swallow before he could force the words out. "I was wrong." A few men raised their brows or grinned. "Yeah, I said it." When they'd all gotten over the shock of Cole admitting he'd made a mistake, he continued. "Jonah is going to stay here, and we're going to have a hell of a fight on our hands."

"My brother blames Cole for making me gay." Jonah's voice was soft but steady.

"Fucking bastard." The words burst from Billy.

"Yeah, he sees recruitment as part of the gay agenda."

Several men laughed.

"Marks is deadly serious though. He was willing to destroy his brother, all but kill him. Think what he'll do to us now that we've brought him back."

Jonah nodded. "If I tell the police, it'll not only out me as gay, but my story will remind everyone that Nathan, my mother, and I are shifters. Nathan hates his animal side. He thinks I'd be damned to hell for using my shifting abilities even if I wasn't gay."

"Fuck." Shep summed up what everyone seemed to be thinking.

Cole sighed. "We're going to get shit dumped on us like never before. So if any of you want to go before the storm, I'll front you two weeks pay, and you can leave with no hard feelings."

Connor stood. "I hate to do this. I… Marks is a bigoted bastard, and the good Lord never intended anyone to treat a kid like that no matter what, but I got kids of my own, and I… shit, I just can't make this my fight."

Cole nodded. "I'll put your pay in the bank today. Let me know if you need a reference."

Silence descended as Connor walked to his truck. The slam of his door echoed across the yard.

Manuel stood next, and Cole's stomach knotted. He was the best groom they had. Cole already envisioned making him assistant trainer when Shep retired even though he'd only worked there a few months.

Manuel made no move toward the bunkhouse though. "You gave me a chance. You believed I could turn my life around when no one else did. You made me feel like family, not some scum you were giving charity to. Now you need me to get your back. Damn right I'm gonna stay."

Before Cole could respond, Rob, another of the hands, a man he'd hired as a nineteen-year-old runaway, stood and said, "I may not get the whole butt sex thing—" He paused until the laughter died down. "But I don't give a goddamn what you do in the bedroom. You're the best boss I've ever had, and I'm staying right here."

Cole's chest tightened as the rest of his men stood too. Shep started clapping; then they all joined in. Cole glanced at Jonah. Shock showed on his face, and his eyes shone. "Thank you," Cole shouted. "Thank you all."

Billy stood on one of the benches. He held up his hands for silence. Despite his being the smallest man there, everyone stopped and looked at him, obviously awaiting his command. His natural leadership never ceased to amaze Cole. "We're going to fight, but we're not going to neglect the farm. So unless Cole and Jonah need us now, let's get our chores done so we can back them up when the sheriff gets here. From now on, I don't want anyone going out alone or unarmed. There's no telling how or when Marks will come after us. But I'm certain he will."

Billy's voice was strong as ever, but he looked shaken. Cole took his unflappable nature for granted, but this time Cole had laid a hell of a load on him.

The men began to scatter toward their morning duties. Cole pulled Jonah into his arms for a tight hug. He slid a hand into Jonah's thick hair and pressed his head onto his shoulder. A wave of hungry lust ran through him. His wolf smelled Demon and wanted to take him down. *Fuck! How was this going to work?*

He looked up, wanting to talk to Billy before he took off, but Billy was already heading for the barn, walking faster than necessary. What was going on with him? Cole had to find out. He didn't need anything else distracting them right now.

"You ready?" he asked Jonah. Jonah nodded against his shoulder. "Good. Let's call Sheriff Trent."

Chapter 6

"So your brother really is a shifter too? That's not just a rumor."

"It's an inherited trait. All my blood relatives are horse shifters, sir."

"Even your mama?" the sheriff looked horrified at the very idea of Agnes Marks taking on a horse form. They might as well have told him she was a stripper.

"She doesn't use her alternate form. I don't even know if she can shift anymore, now she's been human so long."

The sheriff nodded. "And your brother?"

"He'd prefer everyone believed he never changed either."

"But he does?"

"On occasion." Jonah nearly whispered the words. The scent of fear tickled Cole's nose, making his wolf take notice.

"But despite resenting the ability to shift, your brother forced you into horse form and somehow made you stay that way."

Cole snarled. "I don't like your tone, Trent. Jonah suffered a brutal abduction. Just because Marks and his ilk voted you into office, it's still your damn duty to prosecute attempted murder. The man sold his own brother to be tortured and starved."

The sheriff held up his hand. "Calm down, Wilder. Something unsavory has definitely gone down here. I'm going to figure out what it is." He looked at Jonah. "Tell me what happened."

"Nathan punched me. I hit my head, and then he gave me a drug, probably Zenetheldrine. It forces a shape-shifter to stay in animal form."

"How long does it take to wear off?"

"Depends on how much you're given," Cole answered.

"What's the longest?"

"A few weeks."

Trent tilted his head like he was considering something. "Why didn't you shift back then?"

"I'd lost the ability. The longer I was a horse, the less I felt human I-I don't know how to explain it."

"Have you got any evidence to prove you're the horse Wilder bought? Or that you were abused while in horse form?" Trent asked.

Cole growled. "He's not lying, Sheriff."

"Wilder, I need more to go on. I can't go arresting Marks until I have something solid. You know the law does fuck-all to protect shifters right now."

Jonah stood. "Let's go outside."

Cole frowned. "Jonah?"

He looked over his shoulder. "Trust me."

Cole and the sheriff followed him outside. "When I was at the horse rescue, I visited a vet. He took blood samples and cared for the wounds I had. April will have those medical records and also records identifying the man who owned me. You should be able to trace his purchase back to the man my brother dealt with."

The sheriff nodded. "That will help, but—"

Jonah held up his hand. "You want proof I'm the horse Cole adopted. I'll give a blood sample as a human, and you can match it. I'll also give you this." Jonah backed up several steps, and the air around him shimmered. A scrawny roan stallion with scars on his back stood in his place. The clothes Jonah had been wearing lay on the ground, ripped to shreds.

Cole's heart pounded. He knew what shifting cost Jonah.

The sheriff stumbled backward, eyes wide. "Goddamn, I've never seen anything like that."

"See the scars on his back?" Cole gestured toward Demon. "That's what he had to endure thanks to his brother."

"Son of a bitch!" Trent exclaimed. He knew how hard a man had to hit to wound a horse that badly. Trent might be uneasy around shifters and gay men, but he loved horses. He would never defend anyone who harmed them.

Demon stamped his foot and shook his head. Cole went to him and rubbed his nose. "I'm right here. You can come back anytime."

Seconds later Jonah stood in front of him. The color drained from his face. He took a few wavering steps and then bent over, bracing his elbows on his thighs. But this time, he didn't vomit. After a few slow breaths, he straightened and smiled at Cole. "I did it."

"Yep, you did." Cole tossed Jonah his coat, grinning. "And now you owe me a pair of sweats and a T-shirt."

Jonah tied the coat around his waist, making himself decent, then turned to face Trent. "You gonna question my brother now?" Jonah asked.

Trent paled. "Yeah. I've never seen a shifter change before."

"Neither have I," Cole said. The sight was impressive as hell.

Cole smiled at Jonah. He was proud of him, and he wanted to scoop him up and take him to bed. But they had to make sure the sheriff took them seriously. Marks would have a cover story, no doubt. "So you believe us now? You'll talk to Marks?"

Trent nodded. "I will. I'll also send someone out to get a blood sample from Jonah, and we'll get the records from April's Haven."

Cole growled. "I want Nathan to pay."

Trent stared back, unfazed. "I've got to do this by the book. It's not going to be easy no matter how much evidence there is. Marks'll have a lot of supporters in town ready to jump to his defense."

And they'd bring a mess of trouble down on Wild R Farm. "We know."

"You should stick close to home while I check this out."

"We're not going to hide. That's the whole reason we're going through this."

Trent frowned. "Fine, but watch your back. And keep Jonah close."

"If I have my way, he won't leave my sight."

The sheriff blushed, obviously knowing Cole meant that literally, day and night.

"One more thing, Sheriff," Jonah said. He gave Cole a searching look. Jonah believed Nathan would bring up Jonah's interest in Cole, and his belief Cole somehow made Jonah gay. Cole nodded, giving Jonah the go ahead to explain.

"What is it, Jonah?"

"What set my brother off, pushed him over the edge to kidnap me, was a set of pictures he found on my computer."

The sheriff raised a brow. "Pictures?"

"Of Cole."

Trent glared at Cole. "Really."

"Cole didn't know about them. I took them at a horse show. I'd had a crush on him for a long time. But Nathan already had the idea Cole turned me gay."

"And why's that?"

"I asked Cole to hire me a couple of weeks before I disappeared. Maybe Nathan found out, but Cole's the only openly gay man he knows. He had to blame someone. I couldn't have just been born this way. That meant he was 'tainted' too."

Trent let out an exhausted-sounding breath. "I get it." He turned to look at Cole again. "Wilder, when I questioned you about Jonah's disappearance, you didn't say anything about Jonah talking to you. As I recall, you got pissed as hell at me for involving you."

Cole looked at the ground, uncomfortable and embarrassed. "Jonah never said he liked me. He just asked for a job. I had no idea what his brother thought about me."

"You still should've told me he'd been looking for work. It would have been good to know Jonah wanted to get away from his family."

Cole kicked at a pebble. "I was hurt, angry, and stupid. I'm sorry. Can we move on now?"

The sheriff smiled. "Yes, but I mean what I said. Watch your back. Most people have made peace with your presence here. You're known for your horseflesh, and people respect that. But people are easily influenced and there's no way in hell Marks will keep his trap shut about this case. He'll be drumming up support before I'm off his porch steps."

"I've already talked to my men and told them what we're in for. We're as ready as we can be." *But what if it wasn't enough?* If Jonah's owner hadn't died when he did, Jonah might not have survived. Nathan obviously didn't care if Jonah lived or not, and he sure as hell wouldn't mind killing Cole.

Cole put his arm around Jonah and pulled him in for a side hug as they waved good-bye to the sheriff. They were doing the right thing, and they'd made a good start. Jonah might be young, but he was brave and strong, and Cole couldn't love him more.

Love? Wow. He hadn't said the word yet, even to himself. He might not be ready to vocalize it, and Jonah might not be ready to hear it, but he was a wolf in love with his prey. A cowboy in love with his horse. A man in love with a man in a conservative Tennessee town. He'd never been one to choose the easy path.

* * * *

"No! Please! Don't do this! I'm a person!"

Cole sat up. What was going on?

Jonah thrashed beside him, trapped in a nightmare. He'd been with Cole now for over a week, but he still hadn't had a peaceful night's sleep. And neither had Cole.

"Jonah!" Cole shook him gently. "Jonah, it's Cole. You're OK. You're dreaming."

Jonah wouldn't wake up. Cole snuggled next to him, spooning him "Baby, it's OK, wake up. Feel me here with you. It's OK."

Jonah still cried out, begging for his torment to stop. Cole nipped his neck, hoping to wake him.

Jonah tensed. Cole watched him bring up his hand in front of his face. Sweat ran down into his eyes. He brushed it away then stared at his hand. "A dream. Just a dream. I'm… I'm human."

Cole squeezed him. "Yeah, it was just a dream. You're here with me, and you're human."

"Cole?"

"Yeah, baby?"

"Tell me you're real too."

"I am." Cole was a beast for getting turned on when Jonah was so scared, but Jonah's ass wiggling against him had his cock hard as a rock.

His slid an arm under Jonah, pulling him roughly against him, his fingers digging into Jonah's flesh. His wolf wanted possession. Jonah moaned and rubbed his ass against Cole's erection, deliberately this time.

Jonah wasn't going to make it easy to use restraint. Cole licked his neck, tasting the sweat and fear from his nightmare. His wolfish nature wanted to take advantage of that fear. He longed to hold Jonah down while he rode him hard. He wanted Jonah to struggle, to plead. His wolf moved inside him as if trying to burst through his skin. He shoved away from Jonah, scrambling to the far side of the bed.

Jonah rolled over to face him. "What's wrong?"

"No control." Cole's heart slammed against his ribs. It echoed in his cock as blood pumped through the hard flesh. *Take him. Use him. He's yours.* The words echoed in his mind. *No! That's not what Jonah needs now.*

Jonah reached out and took his hand. "Your human side controls the animal. Send him away."

Several seconds passed as Cole tried to do what Jonah said. Finally, he saw his wolf snarl and turn away. He could breathe again. He rolled Jonah onto his back.

Jonah stared up at him and smiled. Cole caressed his cheek with a shaky hand then slid his fingers across Jonah's throat and along his chest. Jonah sucked in a breath as his fingers skimmed Jonah's abdomen and neared his thick cock, which stood up asking for attention.

Cole adjusted his position and took the tip of Jonah's cock into his mouth. He sucked gently on the glans and then ran his tongue around the seam between head and shaft. Jonah moaned and reached for him, sliding his hands into Cole's hair. "More."

Cole couldn't deny him. He took him deeper into his mouth and reached a hand down to tug his balls, pulling almost hard enough to hurt. Jonah bucked his hips, pushing himself down Cole's throat. Cole choked and pulled back.

"Sorry."

Cole smiled. "It's OK. I like you enthusiastic."

He licked Jonah's shaft then swallowed the length of his cock, finding the right angle to take him all the way down this time, loving the feel of the wiry hair at the base of Jonah's cock brushing his face. Jonah made a strangled sound and gripped Cole's head again. "Fuck, that's good."

Cole stayed there as long as he could then pulled back, sucking hard. He slid his mouth up and down on Jonah's shaft and pushed two fingers into his mouth alongside Jonah's cock, getting them good and wet.

He pushed Jonah's legs farther apart and lapped at his balls while circling the tight ring of his anus with his slick fingers. Jonah pushed against him, but Cole held back, teasing him. He pumped Jonah's shaft with his other hand. Jonah squirmed, trying to get what he wanted. Cole looked up. "Do I need to tie you up?"

Jonah shook his head. "No, sir."

Cole shuddered at his submissive words. "Hands over your head. Hold the headboard." Cole loved the feel of Jonah's hands on his face, his strong fingers digging into Cole's scalp, pulling his hair and forcing his head down. But if Jonah played the aggressor now, Cole's wolf would attack. He wanted to pleasure Jonah, to focus on giving him the best orgasm of his life. He didn't want to worry about ripping him apart.

Jonah obeyed slowly as if the action cost him a great deal. He reached for the headboard and gripped the slats. His warm brown gaze never left Cole's. The sight of him stretched out, his cock straining, red and needy, his muscles tense, his eyes full of need and a touch of fear made Cole's cock jump. He longed to bury himself in Jonah's ass again, but he could wait.

When Jonah stilled, Cole pushed a finger inside him. Jonah gasped and arched up, driving Cole's finger deeper. Cole swatted his ass. "Be still."

Cole watched Jonah fight himself. Finally, Jonah held his hips still, but he stayed tense, holding his breath.

"Breathe," Cole touched his chest. Jonah drew in a shaky breath.

"Better." Cole kept his voice low. He moved his finger in and out slowly and pumped Jonah's shaft with the same steady rhythm. Every time Jonah raised his hips seeking more, Cole stopped. His arm shook as he fought to restrain himself, and his cock was so fucking hard it hurt. He couldn't fight his own need much longer.

He tamped down that urge and added another finger to the one in Jonah's ass. He stroked Jonah's prostate, making him whimper but he stayed still. "Good boy." He tightened his hold on Jonah's cock, giving him firmer strokes.

Jonah whimpered again. "Please."

Cole smiled and took Jonah's dick back down his throat. He wanted to draw Jonah's pleasure out until he was soaked with sweat, panting and begging, but he wasn't going to last. He needed Jonah to come now, or he was going to blow his load all over the sheets while he toyed with him.

He used his tongue, a gentle scrape of teeth and every nasty technique he knew to bring Jonah right to the edge. He added a third finger to the two in Jonah's ass, scissoring them, stretching him enough to make his ass burn. Jonah rattled the bed. His breath whooshed in and out in shallow pants. His muscles tensed.

Cole stopped teasing. He sucked hard and fast, tugging Jonah's balls with one hand, burying the fingers of his other hand deep in Jonah's ass. "Fuck. Oh, fuck," Jonah cried, and then he spilled into Cole's mouth. Cole fought his own need to come as he sucked down all of Jonah's fear, his need, his desperation, swallowing it all.

When Jonah was spent, Cole rose up on his knees, took his dick in hand, and pumped himself hard and fast. Seconds later, he came, his first spurt landing on Jonah's face, the rest spilling over his chest and stomach, marking him.

Jonah groaned. "I want to taste it, Cole."

Cole thought he was done, but Jonah's hot words brought on another spasm of his muscles. He milked the last of his orgasm from his cock and sat back. He ran his fingers through the cum on Jonah's chest and brought them to Jonah's mouth. His lover licked eagerly while Cole cleaned Jonah, savoring the taste of his own cum on Jonah's skin.

He reached up and tugged Jonah's hands from the headboard. "Hold me."

Jonah pulled him close, and they kissed. Cole growled as he tasted himself on Jonah's tongue. Jonah squeezed him tighter. The kiss was sweet and hot, desperate and languid, new and achingly familiar all at once.

Cole shuddered. He couldn't deny he loved Jonah. He didn't know if he could say the words yet, but his chest hurt when he thought of this amazing young man beneath him. He wouldn't be able to protect Jonah from all the hurt his brother wanted to inflict on them, but he would do everything he could for him. He would soothe every insult with his hands, his tongue, his cock, and even his heart.

Chapter 7

Cole looked up from flipping pancakes to see Jonah walk into the kitchen. Cole's sensitive nose could smell his soap and shampoo from across the room, but he longed to bury his face against Jonah's neck and breathe deep, filling himself with Jonah's own scent. Jonah's tight jeans clung to his thighs, and the blue shirt he wore made the red in his hair stand out. Cole wanted to strip the clothes off him, sweep the plates off the table and take him right there.

Jonah raised a brow. "We should at least eat breakfast first."

Cole's cheeks heated. "How'd you know what I was thinking?"

Jonah grinned. "I wasn't sure, but I am now."

Cole scowled at him. "Am I really that easy to read?"

"Only when you have that look."

"What look?'"

"The one that says 'The better to eat you with, my dear.'"

Cole growled. "You shouldn't taste so damn good."

Jonah came up behind him and circled his waist. He flicked his tongue up the side of Cole's neck. Cole jerked, nearly burning himself on the edge of the skillet. He growled. "You're dangerous."

"Says the wolf to his prey."

Cole set the spatula down and put his arms on top of Jonah's, trapping him in place. He rubbed his ass against Jonah's cock, getting the reaction he wanted. His own cock grew hard too, as he remembered the wild fuck they'd had before he came down to make breakfast. "Are you always this sassy after a mind-blowing orgasm?"

Jonah laughed. "You love it."

Later, when they'd eaten their fill of pancakes and sausage, Cole tipped his chair back and stared at the ceiling, not wanting to look at Jonah when he announced his plans. "I'm going to head into town today."

Jonah set his coffee cup down with a clunk. "I thought you were going to send Billy or one of the hands on the errands until the Trent gathers enough evidence to arrest Nathan."

Cole considered what to say. He *had* agreed to that, basically to get Jonah to stop worrying and start fucking him one night as they lay in bed. "I know, but I can't hide anymore. I won't let your brother take our freedom."

Jonah stood and walked to the window. He leaned on the counter as he looked out. Cole could tell by the rigid line of his back that he was good and pissed. "You never intended to keep your promise, did you?"

Cole sighed. He really didn't want to have an argument, but he had strong feelings about not letting Nathan Marks dictate where he went and what he did.

Jonah surprised him by laughing. "That's what I get for extracting a promise with your dick in my hand."

Cole grinned, relieved Jonah wasn't yelling at him. "Damn right."

Jonah came back to the table and took a few sips of coffee. Then he set his cup down and looked straight at Cole. "I'm coming with you."

Cole sat up. His chair hit the floor with a bang. "The hell you are."

"You just said we shouldn't hide."

"*I'm* not going to hide. Your brother already tried to kill you once. Don't give him an open target."

"If he was going to shoot me in front of the town, he'd have done it a year ago. It would have saved him a hell of a lot of trouble."

Cole's heart thumped against his ribs so hard he thought they might break. "No."

"Goddamn it, Cole. You can't give a speech about how we shouldn't let Nathan restrict our movements and then tell me I can't go with you."

"What if we run into him?"

The color drained from Jonah's face, but he held Cole's gaze. "I'll smile and say 'hello'."

Cole's gut knotted. Jonah wanted to be brave, but Cole smelled his fear. "You don't have to do this. You have nothing to prove."

"If you're not hiding, I'm not hiding."

"Maybe your brother won't harm you physically in front of witnesses, but he sure as hell won't be shy about sharing his feelings about our relationship. He thinks his alibi is airtight."

"I know. Billy told me what happened when he went to get feed a few days ago."

"Goddamn it! I told him—"

Jonah scowled. "I asked, and he was honest. I have a right to know. You may be older, but I'm an adult whether you see me as one or not."

Cole nodded. As much as he hated it, Jonah was right. He was an adult if a young one. Cole couldn't force him to stay here, but damn it, the thought of seeing Jonah hurt, of listening to his brother spew his hatred in front of Jonah, made the pancakes lay heavy in Cole's stomach. Billy had nearly come to blows with Nathan and his friend Landry after they'd started harassing him for working for the local fag. They'd threatened not to sell to Wild R anymore if Jonah didn't drop "his ridiculous charges". Billy told them he was picking up their order because it was pre-paid. They'd be driving to Weston for their feed from now on.

"Cole?"

He realized he'd been staring at Jonah for several seconds. "OK, you can come. You're right. You're an adult. I can't stop you."

Jonah nodded. "Thank you."

"But you better believe I'm going to come to your defense if anyone starts in on you. You're not fighting this alone."

"I'd rather you fight beside me than for me. I've got to face Nathan myself. If he thinks he can push me around, this will never stop."

"It'll stop when he's rotting in prison."

"We can't count on that happening. Sheriff Trent may never find enough evidence for an arrest, and even if there's a trial, Nathan'll probably get off."

Cole growled. "Anyone who pays attention—"

Jonah's eyes flashed anger. "You know as well as I do paying attention and having sense have little to do with justice in a place like this."

"I know but—"

"He should have to pay, but what's more important is that we have a chance to be together."

"Wow. You do sound like a grown-up."

Jonah flipped him the middle finger. "Fuck off."

Cole laughed, and Jonah smiled at him. "Cole, I…"

Cole's heart beat. He smelled fear. He wanted to scoop Jonah up, take him back to bed, and never let him go.

Jonah looked down at his empty plate and shook his head.

"What?" Cole wanted to know, and yet he didn't. He wasn't sure his heart could take it.

Jonah smiled, but Cole could tell he was covering much stronger emotions. "Nothing."

Tell him. Cole resisted his inner voice. He did love Jonah, but he didn't want to scare him or force something too soon. Jonah was so young. He had his whole life ahead of him. Why would he want to commit to staying at the farm? To staying with Cole?

* * * *

Cole and Jonah stepped out of the bank. Billy was meeting them at Fran's Chicken Shack. After being stared at all morning, Cole could use some greasy chicken and biscuits.

Billy had asked to ride along with them, saying he needed to pick up a few things, but he really wanted to keep an eye on them. He was worried what Nathan or his friends would do if confronted with Cole and Jonah together.

Cole reassured him they weren't going to flaunt their relationship. He might be out of the closet, but he didn't go around town holding hands or kissing on street corners. Not here. He wouldn't pretend he was something he wasn't, but he wouldn't ask for a fight either.

Billy didn't think it mattered. Just seeing them together might make some of these idiots go berserk. He said anyone who would torture his brother the way Nathan had Jonah couldn't be sane. No matter how confident Jonah was that he wouldn't hurt them in front of witnesses, Billy still worried Nathan might just shoot them in cold blood in the middle of town. Cole suppressed a shudder just remembering the conversation. Part of him thought Billy was right. He'd gritted his teeth the whole way into town to keep from begging Jonah to change his mind. He wanted to turn around, drive them home, crawl back into bed and fuck Jonah into submission.

A man never learns anything with his head in the sand. His mother's words echoed in his mind. She was right. She always had been, and after thirteen years he still missed her. She would've wanted him to take care of Jonah. She would've told him to take Jonah in when he'd asked for a job. He'd known that a year ago, but he'd pretended he didn't. His mother would've said Jonah was old enough to stand up for himself and start making his own life, so he was old enough to warm Cole's bed. The thought made Cole smile.

"What?" Jonah looked puzzled, but some of the tension went out of him. Cole was thrilled to know his smile had done that.

"I'm just thinking about how much my mother would have liked you."

Jonah gave a lop-sided smile. "Really? She wouldn't mind that I'm…"

"Young?"

"And a guy."

Cole shook his head. "She knew I was gay, probably before I did. She wanted me to be who I was, a half-breed wolf, a gay man, none of that mattered to her. I was her son, and she loved me."

Jonah shook his head. "Must've been nice."

"Yeah. I just wish she could see me now. She'd laugh like crazy if she knew I was back here where she grew up. She raised me as a city boy. She'd get a kick out of me taking over the farm, a man with werewolf blood training horses."

Jonah snickered.

Heat rose in Cole's cheeks. "Of course, riding one particular horse is a hell of a lot more fun than the others."

Jonah smiled. "I should hope so." He lifted his hat and pushed his hair back before settling it on his head. "But I do reckon you're probably the only werewolf horse trainer in Tennessee if not in the whole country."

"No one can say I don't like a challenge."

"How dare you show yourself in town?" Jonah's brother Nathan stepped out of the doorway of the feed store and blocked their path. Cole hadn't realized they'd gotten so close to the store. He'd meant to be more vigilant, but he'd been caught up in talking to Jonah, watching Jonah, wanting Jonah. And he shouldn't have to worry about where he was. They had just as much right to be in this town as bigoted scum like Nathan Marks.

Jonah tensed. Cole laid a hand on his arm, a feeble attempt to hold him back. Attacking Nathan would not help their case, but right then he wasn't sure he cared.

Jonah's mom stepped out of the store. "Let's not make a scene, Nathan. Come on back inside. It's best if we ignore them."

"How can I ignore them if they're going to flaunt themselves on the street? I thought we were rid of Jonah after he ran off, but now Wilder's brought him back. He's been corrupting the boy for years. Jonah'd never have turned out this way otherwise. He sure as hell didn't learn it from us."

Mrs Marks's eyes shone with tears. She didn't say anything else.

Jonah brushed off Cole's hand. "You know damn well I didn't run off. You drugged me and sold me, you bastard." He lunged toward his brother, but Cole pulled him back.

Nathan stood his ground, looking unaffected. "You know that's not true, Jonah." He looked at

Cole. "Are you really so desperate to sodomize him you had to fill his head with lies, to twist the truth and make him think we'd harm him when we want to help him?"

Cole longed to pound the smug son of a bitch into the dirt. His wolf stirred and this time he wanted to let it loose. But he couldn't end up in jail for assault. Jonah needed him. Somehow he had to hold his temper. He visualized his wolf backing down like Jonah had taught him. "Were you going to help him by killing him?"

"By teaching him to reject sin."

Anger burned in Cole. His wolf clawed at his chest again. "Drugging your brother to force him into animal form isn't a sin?"

Nathan ignored him. "Jonah, you know you've never been as strong as the rest of us. You've always needed my guidance. But there's still hope for you, if you'll fight your demons."

Cole growled. Jonah stood pale and frozen. Cole wanted to tear Nathan apart, then take Jonah home and show him just how perfect he was. He heard footsteps behind him. He turned, ready for a fight and saw Billy. His manager had a talent for diffusing tension. And as much as Cole wanted to rip Nathan apart, he wanted Nathan in prison more.

"Marks, get back in your store and quit harassing my boss."

Nathan turned his bluster on Billy. "You never did tell me what you're doing working with these fags, Carter."

"Why do I care what they do in bed?"

Nathan spat on the dusty sidewalk. "Because it's an abomination. Or are you all a bunch of cocksuckers at Wild R?"

Billy gave a mocking laugh. "Don't knock it. Might improve your personality to have a dick down your throat."

So much for Billy diffusing the situation.

Nathan launched himself at Billy, but Billy landed the first punch. He looked small and non-threatening, but he was strong as an ox. A pound-you-into-the-dirt fight after Cole disparaged Billy's horse had sealed their friendship, and earned Billy the respect he wanted from Cole.

Jonah watched wide-eyed as Billy beat the shit out of Nathan, showing no mercy for Nathan's obvious underestimation of him. Cole was about to pull him off Nathan before he did serious damage, but Billy gave Nathan a final kick and stepped back. Nathan groaned, turning his head to spit blood onto the sidewalk.

"Get back in that store, and be sure to tell everyone you just got your ass kicked by one of the Wild R cocksuckers."

Nathan struggled to get his legs under him. He slipped once then got to his knees. His dark eyes were black with anger. "So he turned you fucking gay too?" He glared at Cole.

"Hell, no, I could probably teach him a thing or two about how to fuck a man. I've been gay as long as I've been alive."

Nathan snarled. "You'll pay for this."

Billy shook his head. "No, you're going to pay for what you did to Jonah."

"I didn't do anything." Nathan had sounded indignant, holier-than-thou. Now he sounded like a petulant kid.

Mrs Marks glared at Nathan. She didn't look the least bit pleased with his behavior.

Nathan mumbled something as he got close to her, but she refused to relent. "Don't look at me for sympathy. I told you to come back inside."

For a moment Cole thought Nathan was going to hit her, but he pushed past her into the store.

Cole wanted to be angry with Billy. As much as his wolf had wanted a piece of Nathan, it would've been better if they'd all stayed out of it. Still, he couldn't help but feel damn proud of Billy for standing up for them and for coming out like that.

He'd suspected Billy was gay when they met. Then he'd run into him at a gay bar in Nashville, but they'd never talked about it. Now with homophobic feelings running higher than they had in years thanks to Nathan and his damn friends, Billy refused to hide who he was. Cole was honored to have him managing the barns at his farm.

Jonah hadn't said a word or even moved through the whole incident. He was pale and frightened. He looked so vulnerable Cole considered dragging Nathan back outside for round two. If only tearing out the bastard's throat would solve their problems.

He touched Jonah's arm. "You OK?"

Jonah nodded, but he still didn't speak. They couldn't talk here anyway so Cole walked over to

Billy who'd just risen from the sidewalk. "What the hell was that?

Billy looked up, eyes hard. "I don't need a lecture from you."

"I'm not going to lecture you. I should, but I'm not."

"I did it for you." Billy's voice quavered as he said the words.

Cole drew in a sharp breath. Billy muttered an expletive and walked away, but not before Cole noticed the longing in his eyes. Now Cole understood why Billy had been acting strange since he'd found Jonah. He saw Billy as a damn good friend, but Billy had apparently started to see him differently. Shit, why hadn't he noticed?

Cole grabbed Jonah's hand and they followed Billy down the street to Fran's.

No one hassled them at Fran's, but plenty of people looked the other way rather than acknowledge them. Cole supposed after Billy's confession, they might be scared his gay would rub off on them too. Jonah hardly said a word during lunch. He looked shell-shocked. Cole wanted to comfort him, but this wasn't the place.

Cole and Billy talked about everything *but* what happened at Marks Feed. They were painfully polite. Cole didn't want to lose Billy, but he had no idea what to say to make things right again. *I never should have come to town.* He could've let Billy take care of everything, but he had to be so goddamn stubborn.

And now Cole knew how Billy felt about him, and Billy knew Cole knew. Would he leave? If Cole had to beg him to stay, he would, because as much as he loved watching Nathan get his ass kicked, they'd brought a load of shit down on themselves. They'd have to be ten times more vigilant now. Billy wouldn't be safe even if he left, and Cole couldn't handle finding another barn manager in the midst of the ensuing storm.

Chapter 8

Billy said good-bye and practically ran to the bunkhouse when they got back. Cole considered going after him, but Jonah hadn't said a word on the drive home. Cole needed to see if he could reassure him first.

Jonah stumbled into the house, and Cole followed him. He could feel the tension radiating from Jonah, and unfortunately, he didn't think a hot fuck was going to ease it. Cole expected Jonah to stop in the kitchen but he kept going to the bedroom. He jerked open a drawer and started pulling out clothes and piling them on the bed.

Cole remembered the day they'd spent in Nashville, shopping for the clothes and other things Jonah needed. Even if Nathan would've let Jonah back in his house, he didn't want to go. He didn't want anything that reminded him of living with a family who saw him as weak and immoral. He had a little money saved from working. One way he stood up to Nathan was insisting on being paid for working in the feed store.

Luckily, the bank manager, Mandy, was one of the few people who'd accepted Cole openly back in high school. After a brief meeting in her office to verify Jonah's identity, she gave him access to his account. Jonah and Cole had shopped for a basic wardrobe for Jonah then enjoyed a delicious dinner and a night of dancing at a club where they were able to let their tension ooze out onto the dance floor. They'd come back to Cranford happy and relaxed.

If only Cole could recapture that feeling now. He grabbed Jonah's arm. "What the hell are you doing?" He hadn't meant the words to come out harshly, but the growl was there in his voice. Fear had him losing control fast.

"What happened today was my fault. When Nathan started hurling insults, telling me what was best for me, I froze like I always have. I fucking hate these instincts that tell me he's the herd leader, and I'm less of a man, not strong enough to challenge him and make a life for myself. He denied what he did to me, and I said nothing." Jonah squeezed his eyes closed and slammed his fist down on the table.

"He's treated you like crap your whole life. And from what I hear, your stepfather was even worse."

"I wish my father had taken me with him when he left."

The sadness in Jonah's voice made Cole desperate to heal him. "I don't."

Jonah looked up, surprise and hurt showing on his face.

"If he had, I would never have met you."

Jonah snorted. "You'd be better off." Jonah pulled open another drawer, taking out more of his belongings.

Fear tied itself into a knot in Cole's belly. "You're not leaving."

Jonah made a noise that sounded like Demon's snuffle of anger. "Yes, I am. I won't be responsible for ruining your business. You've worked hard to earn the respect of people in Cranford, and I know what this farm means to you."

"Jonah, please—"

"You think my brother isn't serious? You think he won't make you pay? He took my humanity, sold me as an animal. You think he won't try to ruin you, even kill you? And after what Billy did to him today, his wrath will be even worse. I can't stay here."

"Billy defended our right to live like we want to. He knew the risk he was taking even if he did lash out in anger. He doesn't want you to leave any more than I do."

Jonah laughed. "Did you see how he looked at you?"

Shit! He didn't think Jonah had caught that. "Yeah. Surprised the hell out of me. Billy's a great friend, but there's nothing more there on my side. I swear. Never has been."

Jonah turned to face him. "I know that. I never thought… I mean, you wouldn't… my point is he fought for you, not for me. He doesn't want to watch this farm go under because of me, and none of the other men do either. You're a savior to most of them. No one else around here would hire them. They love working for you, and there's no way in hell they want to see this farm go under."

"You think they would deny you the same chance they've been given?"

Jonah nodded. "If it brought their world down around them, they would."

Cole hated the way Jonah had been taught to devalue himself, to assume no one cared enough to fight for him. The knot in Cole's stomach tightened. "Would they deny me a chance to find happiness?"

Jonah stared at Cole, considering his words.

Cole held his breath. *Tell him you love him.* Cole ignored the voice of his heart. Not now. Jonah was so unused to love he might run even faster.

Jonah opened his mouth, then closed it, and shook his head. "Not everyone is as generous as you." Jonah picked up some of the clothes, refolding them and stacking them neatly on the bed.

"If you leave, they win—your brother, your mother, your stepdad, all the bigots at that damn church where they preach nothing but hate. They all win. Is that what you want?"

"Goddamn you, Cole. Who's going to win if I stay, and they tear your farm apart? They will keep pounding you until you crumple. There's only so much a man can take. Who wins when they stop with the insults and pull out their guns?"

"You think I didn't deal with the assholes in town when I first took over the Wild R? Half of them wouldn't have a damn thing to do with me. Some of them told me to my face, and some others took it further—cut brake lines, started a fire in the barn. I could have been killed, but I kept going. I fought it. I won a few of them over. The others still hate me, but I'm here running the farm I love."

Jonah looked down. He tugged on the shirt he was holding so hard Cole thought it would rip. "I'm not that strong."

"Yes, you are. You survived almost a year of torture."

Jonah face hardened. "I had no choice. As a horse, I couldn't get away or even just shoot myself."

"God, Jonah. If I think for one minute you're gonna do harm to yourself, I'll tie you to this bed and make damn sure you know how very good it feels to be alive." Cole took a step toward Jonah, but he backed away.

"I might have killed myself if I could have when I was stuck in that barn, starved and hurting, but not now. I don't want to die, but I also don't want to hurt you, and that's what I'll do if I stay here."

Cole growled. "I'll protect you. You are mine, and I'll protect you." His heart pounded. If Jonah left now, he'd never see him again. He had no proof, but he believed it with all his heart. He took another step toward Jonah and held out his hand.

"No." Jonah backed away, bumping into the wall. "This isn't your fight."

Cole took a few more steps toward Jonah. "The hell it's not. I've laid claim to you and I'm going to make your brother pay for what he's done." Cole's voice sounded scary even to himself.

Jonah pressed himself into the wall. "Please. If you touch me now, I won't have the strength to leave."

Cole's chest tightened. He couldn't breathe. His wolf stirred, begging him to do just that. To shove Jonah against the wall, restrain him until he submitted, until he swore he would do whatever Cole asked.

A growl rumbled deep in his chest. Cole took a step back. *No, fuck, no!* He wouldn't hurt Jonah. Jonah's leaving might rip him apart, but he wouldn't force him. No matter what his animal side wanted. He backed up another step. Jonah stayed perfectly still, eyes focused on the floor.

Cole kept moving until he reached the doorway. He didn't trust himself to speak. If he did, he might beg Jonah to stay or tell him off for being so fucking stubborn, or he might just throw back his head and howl.

"I don't have a suitcase," Jonah whispered. His words tore Cole in two. Cole gripped the doorframe to keep from sinking to the floor.

"Please." Cole's word came out strangled, filled with the pain paralyzing him.

Jonah looked up. Tears shone in his eyes.

"Please don't leave," Cole begged.

"I have to."

Cole needed to buy them some time, see if he could think of a way to convince Jonah to stay and decide whether he'd follow Jonah if he insisted on leaving. Would he give up this farm rather than lose the man he loved?

His wolf howled, the sound pounding inside his head. He tightened his hands into fists, nails biting into his palms. Wildness took him. He might be in human form, but he was an animal then, a wounded animal. He stumbled backward, tripping over the raised threshold. "J-just wait… till I… get back.

Jonah wiped at his tears. "Where are you going?"

He tried to speak, but all that came out was a cross between a whimper and a howl. He turned and fled.

His pounding steps took him to the bunkhouse. He jerked the door open, and then slammed it behind him.

Billy turned from where he was filling a water bottle at the kitchen sink. "What's wrong?"

"I-I…" Cole couldn't get enough air in his lungs.

"Sit down." Billy put an arm around him and guided him to the sofa. "Is Jonah hurt?"

Cole shook his head.

"Is anyone hurt?"

Another shake.

"Do you want some water?'

Cole managed a nod this time.

Billy brought him the water. He took it, wrapping a shaky hand around the glass. "P-please don't leave."

"Leave?"

Cole looked up. Billy looked genuinely surprised.

"I just… I thought you might…"

Billy's cheeks reddened. "I'm not leaving."

"I was afraid you would, because…" *I can't finish a single damn sentence.*

Billy grinned despite his embarrassment. "I've had a crush on you for awhile. I knew you didn't feel the same way. I didn't think that had changed. Unless you want me to leave, I'm staying right here."

"So things aren't gonna be weird? You've been tense since Jonah came."

"Yeah, I have. I care for you, Cole. And if I thought I had a chance, I'd make a play for you. I would have a long time ago. It's not been easy seeing you with Jonah or accepting that you're in danger. When Nathan suggested you would rape a boy and corrupt his mind, my feelings boiled over, and I snapped."

Cole's chest loosened. "It's OK."

"Yeah, it is. I want you to be happy. I'm a big enough man to be glad you found somebody who could do that for you. You've been so damn lonely."

"Not too much company around here for a gay man who also has the potential to go berserk and rip your throat out."

Billy laughed. "I rather like the combo."

Cole smiled, but the heaviness returned to his chest when he thought of Jonah. "He's leaving."

"Jonah?'

Cole nodded. "He thinks we don't want to fight for him. He says he shouldn't stay and put us in danger. I tried to make him see reason. I told him we'd be fighting for all of us. If Nathan and his cronies run Jonah off, then who's next?"

Billy nodded. "Did you tell him that?"

"Yeah."

"Exactly that?"

Cole frowned. "No."

"Did you by any chance tell him he was yours and you'd protect him no matter what?"

Heat rushed into Cole's cheeks. *How the fuck does he know me so well?*

"You're a wolf, an alpha wolf, and you think like one. But Jonah needs to be your partner, not a weaker man you have to protect."

"He's so young, and he thinks he's not strong, even though he is."

"He is, and you must think he's a grown-up, or else you wouldn't be taking him to bed."

Cole smiled. "Yeah, he's a grown-up, all right."

"You mean well, but you can be a bit high-handed."

"What do I say? How do I convince him to stay without offering him protection?"

"You tell him what you just told me. You're not just sacrificing yourself to protect him. You're protecting our right to live the way we want. Give Jonah a role in his own defense. He may be young, and he may have been beaten down by his brother, but he's not a damsel in distress. If he thinks all he can do is run and hide, that's what he'll do."

"I fucking hate it when you're right." Cole leaned forward, resting his head in his hands. Billy laughed and patted his back.

Hooves pounded the ground. One of the horses was loose. Or… Cole jumped up and ran to the window, Billy was right behind him. They watched Demon gallop off toward the north.

"Go!" Billy shouted.

"Shouldn't I just let him go if that's what he wants?"

"Playing Alpha Wolf Protector and letting him run off scared and alone with no money or other belongings are not the same thing."

Billy ran out the door and Cole followed him to the barn. Billy quickly fitted Snowdrop with a halter and lead rope. Cole swung up onto Snowdrop's back and held onto her mane.

"Get out of here," Billy said.

Cole looked down at him and regretted for a moment that they'd never had a chance to see where a relationship might go. "I don't deserve you."

"Damn right." Billy slapped Snowdrop's flank, and she took off, nearly unseating Cole.

Chapter 9

Cole clung to Snowdrop's back as she flew over the fields. *How the hell am I going to catch up with Jonah?*

Snowdrop crested a small hill and Cole saw Demon eating clover along the fence line. The horse glanced up but showed no sign of intending to run.

Cole slipped from Snowdrop's back and unhooked the lead rope. She wouldn't go far.

Demon looked up and whinnied. His body reformed too fast for Cole to see. In less than a second, Jonah stood in front of him.

"I asked you to wait for me." The words came out angry and accusatory.

"I needed to clear my head. Going for a run used to be the only way I could do that, the only time I felt free. I wasn't sure I'd ever be able to run as a horse again, but I can. I did. And it felt damn good. I wasn't going to leave as Demon. I would've come back to say good-bye."

Everything Billy said left him in a rush, replaced by his wolfish instincts. Jonah was his, and he was going to keep him.

Jonah scowled. "Did you come out here to drag me back? Were you going to throw me over your horse and ride off with me?"

Anger exploded in Cole. "I came out here to make you see sense."

"I can't give you what you want. When I see Nathan, I want to run as fast and as far as I can. I can't let you fight in my place."

Cole fought past the need to protect, to possess. Desire rose hard and fast as soon as he saw Jonah standing in front on him, naked and sweaty. "What if we fight together?"

Jonah shook his head. "You saw how Nathan affects me."

"So you froze the first time you saw him after he tried to kill you, so what?"

"I only stood up to him a handful of times in my whole life."

"You survived torture that would have killed a lot of men, or at least forced them to take refuge in insanity, and now you're making a new life for yourself. You are the strongest man I've ever met. We can fight this."

"I can't."

Sadness hit Cole like a blow. "Yes, we can. You're so much stronger than me."

"How can you say that?"

"Because I need you so damn much, I'm ready to get on my knees and beg you to stay."

"Cole." Jonah whispered his name. It floated away on the hot wind.

Cole growled. The sound was low, sensuous, a sexual call to another wolf.

Jonah took a step back. His cock hardened, reaching up. Cole licked his lips at the sight of the thick, needy shaft.

Cole's body tightened as Jonah's desire washed over him. Fucking wouldn't solve their problem, wouldn't make Jonah stay, but Cole had to touch him. He had to drive into him one last time before he could let him go. "Stroke your cock." His voice was low and gravelly.

Jonah shuddered and his cock stiffened more. Cole loved that his commanding tone turned Jonah on.

Jonah pumped his dick slowly, hand sliding all the way from base to the tip.

"Do you think about me when you touch yourself?" Cole asked, dropping his hand to rub himself through his jeans.

Jonah nodded.

"Do you think about anyone else?" Cole needed to be the only man he wanted.

"No," Jonah replied, his voice strained with need.

"You're mine." Cole could almost hear Jonah's heart slamming against his chest. He smelled Jonah's fear, his desperation. He walked around Jonah, a wolf circling his prey. "Do you want me now?"

Jonah nodded. "Yes." The word was low, husky, full of desire with a hint of fear.

Cole growled, a savage sound. "I won't hold back if I take you now."

Jonah met his gaze, moving his hand faster on his cock. "Make me remember this."

Cole snapped. He pulled Jonah to him, crushing him against his chest. He took Jonah's mouth, tasting ferocious need in Jonah that matched his own. Jonah would remember this all right, every single day for the rest of his life. If he walked away,

Cole wanted to be sure he would never forget this aching need. Because maybe, just maybe, he'd come back for more.

Cole jerked his shirt off, needing skin-to-skin contact, wanting to push himself, his need, right into Jonah's cells. Their chests rubbed together as he splayed his hands across Jonah's back and licked at the dried sweat on Jonah's neck.

"Need you." Jonah breathed the words into Cole's mouth.

"Yes." Cole ground against him. He wanted to lock himself to Jonah, fuse them together to give and take until they erupted with pleasure. He wanted to feel every inch of Jonah's smooth white skin, to taste the warm depths of his mouth, the salt of his sweat, the musky tang of his cum. Need and emotion beat at his insides. The world spun before him, and he dropped to his knees, pulling Jonah down with him.

Cole pushed Jonah backward until he sprawled on the ground with Cole between his legs. Then he drew Jonah's arms above his head and held them there as he kissed his way along the tight muscles of his neck and sucked on his collarbone. He buried his face in the crook of Jonah's arm, breathing deep of his scent—sunshine, hay, and horse. He sucked on the tender skin under Jonah's arm.

Jonah struggled under him. "Cole!"

Cole couldn't let him go. He needed him right there, spread out like a feast. "Mine," Cole murmured as he drew one of Jonah's nipples into his mouth, using tongue and teeth to make him cry out. He gave Jonah's other nipple the same treatment, pinching the one he'd been sucking. Jonah writhed under him, babbling, begging, but Cole's mind was too lust-clouded to comprehend anything beyond the pure pleasure of Jonah's taste and scent.

He licked his way down Jonah's stomach and tasted the pre-cum leaking from his cock. He shuddered at the taste, like a concentrated version of Jonah's scent. "Don't move." He let go of Jonah's arms and pushed his thighs onto his chest.

"I want to touch you," Jonah pleaded.

Cole shook his head. If Jonah touched him with his tender hands, he might fall apart. He could drive Jonah crazy with need, make him come so hard he'd see stars, make him long to feel this good for the rest of his life, but he couldn't bear Jonah's tenderness knowing he might leave.

"Can't. Just let me give you this."

Jonah struggled under Cole's grip. "Cole, please."

"No." The word came out frighteningly close to a sob.

Jonah whimpered. "I need to taste you, smell you."

Cole pushed his face between Jonah's legs, flicking his tongue across Jonah's anus, cutting off his ability to form words. He attacked Jonah's tight entrance with vigor, pushing his tongue past the ring of muscle. Jonah cried out, arching up and driving him deeper. He stroked Jonah's shaft as he tongue-fucked him, slicking him and opening him up. He needed Jonah ready. He might die if he waited much longer to shove himself into Jonah's tight ass.

Jonah writhed, but Cole held him down. "I'm so close I'm gonna come if you don't stop."

Cole squeezed the base of his shaft and sank his teeth into the one of Jonah's ass cheeks. Jonah screamed. Cole sucked on the flesh in his mouth and licked the wound. His wolf roared to life, wanting blood, begging him to rip Jonah's flesh apart.

Terrified, he pushed away, scrambling back on the grass. *No. God, no! I love Jonah. I won't hurt him.*

"Cole?" Jonah sat up, staring at him with wide eyes. "What is it?"

Cole slid further away.

"What's wrong?'

"My wolf. I can't control it."

"Yes, you can."

Cole couldn't think clearly. His animal needs threatened to overwhelm him.

Jonah scooted closer to Cole. "I'm not afraid."

Cole breathed in his scent and shuddered. "You are. I smell it."

"I'm no more afraid than I want to be."

Bite. Take. His wolf snarled. Jonah liked it rough, but he didn't want to be literally eaten. A growl escaped. His wolf seemed ready to split Cole's skin. "Jonah, run!"

Jonah moved closer, crawling across the grass toward Cole.

Cole trembled and backed farther away like a feral animal scared to be touched.

Jonah stopped moving, but he showed no sign of leaving. "I want you, all of you, even the scary monster you keep locked inside."

Cole's control was melting. The heat of his need taking over. "Please," the word was a plaintive whine, like a wolf in pain.

"Let go. Your wolf needs to roam free."

Cole heard the blood pounding in his ears. *Let me go*. His wolf caressed him with soft fur. *No!*

Jonah didn't understand. Jonah's stallion just wanted to run. He didn't force Jonah to eat people he loved. "No," Cole gasped, finding his human voice. "I'll hurt you."

Jonah shook his head. "You won't. You'll keep your human senses."

"No!" Cole's chest tightened. He couldn't breathe.

"Stop fighting." Jonah's firm words shocked him out of his panic. "Good. Now lay back."

Cole obeyed Jonah, no longer able to resist. His wolf snarled for him to take charge, but he ignored it.

He thought Jonah's touch would make the pull of his wolf stronger, but Jonah's hands sliding up Cole's chest soothed him, made him more human. Even when Jonah teased his nipples, making him gasp, he held his wolf back.

Jonah leaned down and placed a kiss right in the center of Cole's chest. His heart sped up and he thought he might die of wanting, but he didn't dare move for fear the wolf would take control again. "I want you so much." He whispered the words in a hoarse voice.

Jonah smiled. "I know." Jonah spit into his hand and coated Cole's cock with his saliva.

Cole shuddered. Jonah's cool hand did nothing to assuage the burning heat of his shaft. He tore at the grass under him, fighting the need to flip Jonah over and drive into him.

Jonah straddled him and used a hand to guide Cole's cock to his entrance.

Cole tensed. He didn't want to lose control when he was inside Jonah. "I'm not—"

Jonah brushed the tip of his cock back and forth over the tight pucker. "We need this."

Primitive need gripped Cole. His wolf snarled. "I'll hurt you."

"You're controlling yourself right now. Even when I'm—" Jonah sank down just enough to take the very tip of Cole's cock inside him. "About to sit on your cock."

"But I can't—"

Jonah cut his words off by sinking down farther.

Cole groaned as his cock disappeared into Jonah's tight, hot body.

Jonah groaned as he sank lower.

Cole watched his face. Pleasure. Pain. Need.

Jonah smiled and slid down until his ass brushed Cole's balls. He seated himself, gripping Cole's hips with his thighs. "Mmm. So full."

His sexy words brought Cole's wolf roaring to life. He grabbed Jonah's hips as he thrust up, driving himself even deeper.

Jonah gasped. "Your eyes."

"What?" Cole didn't wait for an answer. His need for friction was too great. He lifted Jonah and brought him back down hard enough to make him cry out.

Jonah twisted his hips, sending fiery pleasure through Cole. "Your eyes. They're yellow."

"No! I can't change."

Jonah worked himself up and down. Cole fought the urge to reach for his neck, pull him down, and bite. He held Jonah's hips in a bruising grip and thrust into him again and again.

"Yesss," Jonah cried.

"Did my… eyes… really change?"

Jonah nodded. But he kept riding Cole, working his hips in a way that made Cole crazy. His cock rubbed against Cole, and Cole reached between them to wrap a hand around it. He cupped the back of Jonah's neck with the other hand, trapping Jonah against him so he could taste every inch of his mouth. He was so damn hungry. But he would not bite.

He let Jonah's mouth go and kissed his neck, breathing deep in that place just below his ear where his scent was so strong, taking in the bright, sunshiny smell that drove Cole insane.

Cole flicked his tongue over the spot where Jonah's pulse thrummed. His wolf roared to life.

Jonah tensed as if he sensed danger. He pulled away and rose up off him. Cole dug his hands into the dirt, fighting his raging need. Would Jonah run now?

Jonah positioned himself on his knees, resting his weight on his forearms, displaying his ass.

"Fuck me, Cole. As hard and deep as you can. Fill me with your need."

Cole couldn't have denied him for anything. He rose up over him and drove deep, shoving Jonah forward. His face slid across the dirt, but Cole didn't slow down. He pistoned Jonah's ass, scared he was hurting him, but Jonah pushed back, taking it all. "Yes, Cole. Give us what we need."

Jonah tried to rise up on his arms again, but Cole pushed him down, holding him against the ground with a hand between his shoulder blades. If Cole got any closer he was going to bite, and he wasn't sure he wouldn't rip out some flesh. He dug his fingers into Jonah's hips. Need screamed through him. He threw back his head and howled.

Jonah gasped and shuddered under him, coming without touching himself. Cole came seconds later, buried deep inside him.

When every last spasm of Cole's climax had passed, he pulled out of Jonah and collapsed on the ground, drained of anger, fear, and wolfish hunger. Jonah lay flat on his belly, his back rising and falling with each, shaky breath. Cole reached out and caressed his back. He'd never get enough of just touching Jonah.

Jonah turned his head and looked at Cole. "Feel better?"

Cole held Jonah's gaze. "Are my eyes…?"

Jonah smiled. "Human? Yes. For now, but you're also a wolf, and you have to embrace it."

"But I could kill you." He hadn't, but several times, he'd dangled over the pit of hell by a single finger, destined to fall.

"You've got to accept what's inside you."

"But how?"

"If I need my horse form, I imagine myself on four legs, see my horse in my mind. The change comes when you relax, not when you force it."

"But I can't become a wolf. I've never—"

Jonah shrugged. "Your eyes changed today."

Cole's heart pounded. Could he? He'd tried so hard to change when he was younger. Most shifters gain the ability as they go through puberty, but half-breeds rarely shift. He'd made friends with some wolves when he was in college. He'd done stupid things and taken crazy risks trying to force a change, wanting to be like them. He wanted desperately to be one or the other, wolf or human, not pulled in both directions.

He looked up at Jonah and saw concern in his eyes. "Don't go." The words were out before he could stop them.

Jonah reached for him, pulling him close. "I'll stay a little longer. You need me."

He did, so much it frightened him.

Chapter 10

The next five days passed uneventfully. Cole and Jonah avoided talking about Sheriff Trent's investigation or Jonah's future. They focused on the workings of the farm and primarily communicated with their bodies. Every chance they had to be alone, they came together savagely, tearing at each other, biting, marking, sucking until they were ready to explode. Then Cole drove into Jonah, possessing him while Jonah begged for more. He begged Cole to claim him even as he refused to commit to staying at Wild R Farm.

Then as the sun was setting one evening, Billy charged into the house. "Goddamn bastards."

Cole looked up from the stove where he was giving his spaghetti sauce a taste test. A chill ran over him. "What is it?"

"Fence has been cut in the north pasture. We're missing Star, Angel, and Rory."

Cole squeezed his eyes closed and took a long, slow breath. He'd been waiting for something like this. He'd actually expected worse. "Take everyone you can round up and look for them."

"Sure thing, Boss. Jonah's out repairing the gate to the secondary ring. I…"

"Alone?"

"Yeah. He insisted he was fine."

"Goddamn it!" Cole's stomach lurched at the thought of Jonah out there alone. He grabbed his phone and called Jonah. The phone went straight to voicemail. Cole tried again. There were a few places on the far reaches of the property where their phones lost signal but Jonah shouldn't be near one. Cole's heart raced. He shivered even as hot anger burned in his gut.

"No answer?" Billy asked.

Cole shook his head. "I've got to go after him. If Nathan was willing to kidnap and sell him once, he'd do it again."

"We need the trucks, but I'll saddle Snowdrop for you." Billy took off for the barn.

Cole turned off the stove and grabbed his boots. When he got to the barn, Snowdrop was nearly ready. Billy could tack up a horse faster than anyone he'd ever met, and he'd never appreciated it more.

"I'm sure he's fine." But Billy looked worried and almost nothing ruffled him.

"Yeah, he's got to be." Cole tapped Snowdrop's sides with his heels. As soon as they were on the road, Cole urged Snowdrop into a canter. He rode toward where Jonah was working, moving as fast as he dared.

Please let him be OK. Please let him be OK. He begged any deity who would listen. His stomach churned, nausea tightening his throat. *Faster, faster.*

He crested a hill and saw Jonah, bent over the broken hinge on the gate connecting the secondary ring to the pasture. Fear turned to anger in an instant.

Jonah turned and lifted a hand to shield his eyes from the setting sun. He waved, apparently oblivious to Cole's rage. *How dare he not answer his phone and scare the shit out of me?*

Cole reined in Snowdrop and jumped from her back, barely stopping to tie up the reins as he stomped toward Jonah.

"What's up?" Jonah frowned.

Cole didn't bother to keep the growl from his voice. "Why the fuck didn't you answer your phone?"

Jonah frowned and pulled his phone from a pocket in his denim jacket. "Battery's dead."

"You don't ride out alone without a way to get in touch with me." Cole squeezed his fists to keep from grabbing Jonah and shaking some sense into him.

Jonah scowled as he shoved the phone back into his pocket. "Is that the rule for all the hands or just the ones who can't take care of themselves?"

"It's the rule for anyone whose family would like to see them dead."

Jonah turned back to the fence and checked his work. "I didn't let the battery run down on purpose."

Cole couldn't believe he wasn't taking this seriously. "Can't you be responsible enough to charge your fucking phone?"

Jonah faced Cole, angrier than Cole had ever seen him. "Goddamn it, Cole. Either you treat me with the same respect you give everyone else, or I'm getting the hell out of here. I—"

"Someone cut the fence in the north pasture. Three of our horses are missing."

Jonah relaxed his fighting stance, suddenly seeming several inches shorter. "And you thought—"

"I thought they'd gotten you too."

Jonah nodded. "I'm sorry."

Cole should apologize for attacking Jonah, for treating him like a kid, but the cold fear mixed with anger was hard to let go. "We need to get back to the barn, and do the evening chores while everyone's out rounding up the strays."

"OK. I'll grab the tools." Jonah stood still for a few seconds, looking like he wanted to say more. But he didn't. He just put his tools into Betsy's saddle bags and mounted her.

Cole leapt onto Snowdrop, and they rode off in silence. Cole urged Snowdrop into a canter, knowing Jonah would lag behind. He couldn't go faster than a trot with the heavy tools in the saddle bags. He still didn't trust himself to talk to Jonah. The chance he would say something stupid was too high.

When he reached the barn, he slid from Snowdrop's back and started untacking her. He heard Jonah come in, but he ignored him, focusing on Snowdrop instead. Jonah watched him, but he didn't know what to say. He sucked at making amends. Part of him wanted to just pull Jonah into his arms and kiss him. He should be thankful Jonah was all right and leave it at that, but he hesitated. Something seemed to have shut down between them.

He heard Jonah whispering to his horse, speaking in some special language they shared.

Cole glanced at him, and his breath caught. Jonah was so beautiful, and Cole loved him so much. *Why can't I just say it? Because I haven't since Mama died? Because I'm scared?*

By the time he'd gotten Snowdrop back in her stall, the silence in the barn was thick enough to choke him. Jonah started feeding the other horses. Cole was about to say he'd go check the animals in the other barn when his phone rang. He pulled it from his pocket. Billy's name showed on the display. He answered. "What's up?"

"We found all the horses. None of them had gotten too far."

"Great."

"Shep and Rob are going to see if they can repair the fence before all the light goes. The rest of us are heading back in."

"Sounds good. Jonah and I are back at the barn."

"He's OK?"

"Yeah, his battery died. That's why he didn't answer."

"And you yelled at him for it."

Cole refused to respond.

Billy laughed.

"Is that all?" Cole's voice was cold. He wasn't in the mood to be teased.

"Yeah… no…"

"What? More insults?" Cole snapped.

"I wouldn't think you'd be that touchy after finding Jonah. Are you sure everything's all right?"

"Yeah, we're fine. Just get on with it." Cole tried to sound polite but failed. He was a wounded wolf, and he wanted to go crawl in a hole by himself.

"Find me tonight if you need to talk."

Cole made no response.

"Something doesn't seem right about how easily we found the horses. They were all together just down the road. Makes me think something else is up, or the bastards had another target."

Fear overshadowed anger again. "Do you think someone was waiting, hoping Jonah would come looking for the horses since they were more likely to come to him if they were scared?"

Billy sighed. "Could be. Keep Jonah close, and don't let your guard down."

"OK." Cole ended the call and turned to Jonah who was listening and trying hard to look like he wasn't.

"They found the horses."

"Thank goodness."

"Just don't go off alone again." Why the hell did he say that? People said he was civilized for a werewolf, but he was beginning to think they were wrong.

Jonah frowned. "Cole—"

"I don't ever want to be that scared again." Emotions swirled in him. He was angry at himself, at Nathan, at this culture that rejected anyone who was different—gay, shifter, it didn't matter. His wolf snarled, wanting control. He wanted to hurt someone, to tear something apart.

Jonah surely sensed the danger, but he didn't back away. He stood his ground like a stubborn stallion ready to do battle. "Let me go, Cole. You won't have to be scared if I'm not here."

Cole's stomach churned. "No."

"Today some horses got loose. You found them, but what will happen next? I don't want you to live in constant fear."

Why couldn't Jonah understand Cole's concern for him? He loved his horses and would do whatever it took to protect them, but he cared about Jonah far more. Nathan and the rest of those homophobic assholes could attack the farm. They could even come after Cole himself, but not Jonah. He would never let them hurt Jonah. "You don't get it, do you?"

Jonah looked at him, pain in his eyes. "I get that my being here is hurting you and everyone else on this farm."

But his not being here would tear Cole in two. "I thought they'd taken you. If they forced you back into horse form, you might not survive this time. *That's* what hurt me, the thought of you not being here. All my people agreed to fight this. We—"

"I can't stand to stay here and watch you get hurt because of me. Nathan's been a bully his whole life. He's not going to change now."

"Running away won't solve anything."

"Running is the only way I know to keep you safe."

"Horses run. It's their only defense, but you're more than your animal instincts. You can choose to stay and fight."

"Like you can choose not to be a wolf, like you can stop yourself from sinking your teeth into me?"

Cole took the words like a punch in the gut. He'd let go with Jonah in a way he never had with anyone else. He'd thought Jonah wanted him too. He'd begged Cole to claim him, to bite him. Cole ran from the barn, certain he was going to be sick.

"Cole!" Jonah shouted after him, but Cole ignored him. He had to get away. The world shattered in front of him as if the sky were ripping apart.

Billy pulled up in one of the trucks and jumped out.

"Cole?" Billy stepped in front of him, trying to stop him.

Cole barreled past him, stumbling past the house, into the stand of trees by the stream on the far side of the barn. Cole leaned over, bracing his hands on his knees. His stomach heaved, but his body wouldn't give him the release of vomiting.

He needed to run, to chase, to rip something apart. His wolf raged, clawing at his insides. He froze. He could see himself changing, just the way Jonah described it. He could see his wolf form, but he couldn't quite reach it. He kicked the closest tree trunk. Then he slammed his fists into it, over and over, barely noticing the bark ripping his skin. He screamed with the need to release the animal inside him then sank to his knees from the force of the pain.

What the fuck was he doing? He should have helped Jonah leave like he wanted. He could have just said Demon escaped. No one would've doubted him.

But then he would have left a scared boy on his own with no one to help him. Just like he had a year ago. *God, this agony is going to rip me apart.*

Danger. Cole stood, looking around. He smelled Bruce Landry, one of Nathan's friends. He ran toward the barn, toward Jonah. His vision shifted. He'd bet his eyes had changed like they had when he'd been with Jonah by the stream. Despite the growing dark, he could clearly see Landry creeping around the side of the barn. The fucking bastard had a rifle. Jonah stepped from the barn, right into Landry's line of sight. "No!"

Cole howled. His body shook. He saw the animal inside. Then he became it. Suddenly he was running on four legs with a speed he'd only dreamed of.

Landry gasped and pointed the gun at Cole.

He leaped, knocking Landry to the ground before he could shoot. He closed his mouth around Landry's throat ready to tear it out.

Landry screamed like a man possessed.

"Cole! Cole! Let him go. Killing him won't help me."

That voice. He understood it, but not like he did as a human. He wanted to kill this man, to eat him alive. *Protect the pack. Protect my mate.*

"Cole. Back away."

He forced himself to let go and backed up a few steps. Landry looked at him, face pale, bloody gashes leaking red onto his neck.

Billy stepped forward, pistol trained on Landry. "Sheriff Trent's on his way."

Cole watched Billy, letting the words sink into his wolf brain. Then he looked at Jonah.

Jonah smiled at him. And suddenly, more than anything, he wanted to wrap his arms around Jonah and forget all the anger between them. With that thought, he was human again.

He stared down at his human hands. "I changed."

Jonah smiled. "You did."

Cole glanced back at Landry. Danielle was tying his hands as expertly as she'd once tied calves in the rodeo. Billy still held a gun on him. Landry looked white and cold as snow except for the jagged wound on his neck. *Did I really do that?*

He turned back to Jonah, not wanting to think about how much his wolf enjoyed sinking his teeth into the man.

"I'm sorry I scared you," Jonah said, his words soft.

"Doesn't matter. Nothing matters except you being alive." Cole took a step toward Jonah.

Jonah reached for him and pulled him into a tight embrace. They held each other for several long minutes then Cole pulled back, sadness settling over him again. "Are you leaving now?"

Jonah shook his head. "No."

Cole's chest burned. He stared at Jonah not able to believe what he'd said. "No?"

"No." Jonah's handed Cole his jacket so he could cover himself. Until that moment he hadn't even realized he was naked.

Jonah took his hand and led him to the porch. They sat on the steps, letting Billy and the others handle tying up Landry and making their own interrogation before the sheriff arrived.

Jonah squeezed Cole's hand. "When Landry pointed that gun at you, I understood how you feel. The need to protect you had me ready to rip the man apart with my hands. I nearly shifted and ran him down. If I'd had a gun, I would've shot the son of a bitch. I couldn't let him hurt you."

Cole nodded, too shocked to say anything. *Was I really a wolf?*

"You're right. This isn't just about me. Nathan isn't going to stop now if I walk away. I think I can find the strength to fight, but after seeing you nearly get shot, I don't have the strength to walk away from you."

Cole reached for Jonah, but Jonah resisted. "I need to say this. And if I touch you, I'm not going to be able to focus. Nathan got all the praise growing up. I got blamed for everything that went wrong and for just being me. I never thought I was good enough for anyone, and that was before I realized I was gay. I already knew my family didn't like me. My liking guys would only turn dislike to hatred. I thought about running away. I thought I might not be able to live with myself."

The idea of Jonah's vibrant personality being snuffed out because he wasn't valued by the sick fucks who had raised him made Cole's gut burn. If Nathan had been the one sitting on the ground surrounded by Cole's men, he might have killed him.

"Then I started seeing you at the store, and I got the idea that maybe I could live on your farm."

Cole eyes stung with unshed tears. He couldn't fucking cry in front of his hands. "I'm so sorry. I'll never be able to make it up to you, but I'm sorry."

Jonah smiled and squeezed Cole's hand. "It's OK. You didn't know. I'm not saying this to make you feel guilty."

"I knew you were miserable. That should have been enough."

"It doesn't matter. We're together now, and we're going to fight together. I've finally truly decided I deserve to be free from Nathan and his influence over me."

"I love you." The words tumbled out of Cole's mouth. He'd been so damn scared to say them. He'd tried to force them out a few times. He thought when he worked up the courage it would be painful, but nothing had ever felt so right.

Jonah grinned. "I love you too. I have since I came back but—"

"Me too. I was scared to say it, scared to feel it, scared it wouldn't work."

"It works. It works so damn well."

They came together then. Their kiss was gentle at first, but passion rose hard and fast.

"Cole. Cole!"

Cole registered Billy's voice through a haze of lust. He pulled away from Jonah, turning to see Billy still holding a pistol on Landry. The sheriff was pulling into the driveway.

Billy grinned. "Can you two take it to the farmhouse after the sheriff leaves?"

Heat rose in Cole's cheeks. "Sorry."

Billy laughed. "We'll forgive you this once."

Cole caught Danielle rolling her eyes before she said something in a low voice to Landry and walked over to join them by the porch.

Chapter 11

Landry insisted he'd acted on his own. Cole didn't believe him. He was sure Nathan had put him up to coming after Jonah. The sheriff said he'd be making inquiries. He took statements from Billy, Jonah, Cole, Danielle, and the men who'd ridden up in time to witness the end of the altercation. Then Trent took Landry away to make official charges at the station.

Once they left, Cole talked with Billy, Danielle, and the others about how they could best protect themselves and the horses. He talked fast and took little time for questions. The adrenaline rush of changing for the first time, coupled with Jonah agreeing to stay, had him horny as hell. He needed to get Jonah inside as fast as possible and fuck his brains out.

When everyone else headed off to the bunkhouse to eat supper, Cole grabbed Jonah's hand and half-dragged him into the house. They barely made it into the kitchen before lust overtook them. They shed their clothes the second they got the door closed. Cole lifted Jonah up on the table, taking him hard and fast. They rubbed and pressed against each other as if neither of them could get close enough. Their loving was urgent, wild, filled with the threat of loss and the thankfulness that each of them was still alive.

Afterward, Cole carried Jonah to bed. They snuggled under the covers. Cole lay half on top of Jonah with his head pillowed on Jonah's chest as if his weight could keep Jonah with him. He still couldn't believe Jonah intended to stay. He'd been so sure Jonah would leave since Landry's attack proved him right. They were all in deadly danger.

Jonah stroked his back slowly. "How did it feel?"

"What?" Cole asked, lost in his own concerns.

"Changing." Jonah chuckled.

The sound vibrated through Cole. He flattened his hand against Jonah's chest, feeling his heart beat.

"Strange and yet…"

"What?"

"So natural. I didn't try. It just happened. Same thing when I came back into human form."

"The transformation is easy when you don't force it. Do you feel different?"

Cole let his thoughts slide along his body. Despite the threat to his and Jonah's lives, he could relax in a way he hadn't in years—maybe ever— because the anxiety that nearly always plagued him was gone. So was the underlying anger, and the need to rip something apart. He didn't feel weak, but he didn't have a driving urge to prove himself hammering at his brain. "I do. I feel more… comfortable."

Jonah smiled. "Good. You needed to be fully wolf before you could be comfortable just being human. When the wolf can't come out, the two forms struggle for dominance."

"How do you know that?"

"It's what happens to every shifter when we gain our animal form at puberty."

"Goddamn, you have to go through being a teenager and this… this animal mayhem?"

Jonah grinned. "Oh, yeah. It's teenage hell times ten."

Cole propped himself on his elbow. "You think I could've become a wolf years ago if I'd stopped trying so hard?"

Jonah shrugged. "Maybe, but it doesn't matter. You changed when you needed to." He studied Cole for a few seconds, like he was trying to decide whether to say what was on his mind. "Could you do it again now? Without the fear motivating you?'

Cole's heart pounded. He didn't know. He was afraid of what might happen if he tried. What if he couldn't control the needs of his wolf? "Is it safe to try?"

"Don't try. Feel."

Cole stood from the bed, his body ignoring his mind's protest.

Jonah gave him a slow once over and smiled seductively. "Show me your wolf."

He couldn't deny Jonah's request. He threw his head back and his body dissolved, becoming the wolf. He breathed in. His sense of smell was better than average in his human form, but as a wolf, it was incredible.

He not only detected Jonah's scent, but he could have broken it down into dozens of different underlying notes. To his wolf that smell *was* Jonah, his very essence, and it smelled delicious.

Hunger hit him so hard, his canine legs shook. His tongue hung out of his mouth as he panted. His body quivered with the need to chase. He wanted to eat Jonah, but there was enough humanity in his wolf's brain to tell him his true hunger was for sex not food. And then there was the tactile craving to simply rub against Jonah and draw his scent deep into the fiber of Cole's wolf's body.

Jonah stared down at him. "Do you feel our connection?"

He whined and yelped, an embarrassingly submissive sound.

"Your wolf smells me, but he labels the smell as sex and love."

Cole nodded, wishing he could answer.

"I feel it too when I'm in horse form. My horse senses danger when you're around. I know you're a predator, but you smell like pleasure, like a need so deep I can't describe it, like the fulfillment of every desire I've ever had."

Cole nodded and yelped again. Jonah understood perfectly.

"You're not going to attack me. You are a wolf but your needs are still human, and you need me like a man."

Cole nodded. Did he ever. He wanted to regain his human form and take exactly what he wanted, but he didn't attempt to change form. Jonah hadn't asked him to, and instinctively he knew, alpha wolf or not, he wasn't the one in control tonight.

"Good." Jonah wrapped his hand around his cock and stroked slowly. Cole watched as Jonah's cock hardened, growing long and thick until it stood straight out from his body. "Do you want me?"

Cole's canine heart thumped against his ribs faster than his human one ever could. This aggressive side of Jonah was driving him wild.

Cole yipped, trying to tell Jonah he wanted him more than anything.

Jonah grinned, still touching himself. "Good. Your wolf is beautiful, but I need you human now."

Cole breathed in and let the warmth of Jonah's words rush over him. Effortlessly, he became human again.

Jonah looked up and down Cole's body like he was studying a sculpture. "Beautiful!"

Cole shook his head. He was proud of his body, but he was too big and hairy to be beautiful.

Jonah gave that alluring smile again, the one promising mind-blowing pleasure. Cole was thankful for his shifter stamina and Jonah's. His dick was hard and ready to go again despite the fact he'd pounded Jonah into the kitchen table not long ago.

Jonah tugged harder on his cock. "Get on the bed."

Cole bristled. He didn't take orders. His alpha instincts told him to protest, but some secret part of him wanted exactly what Jonah had planned. He needed to know he could submit. If he could let Jonah fill his ass with that thick cock without snapping, then he was more than the sum of his animal needs.

"Please let me do this."

"OK." Cole's voice was low, strained. He wanted Jonah too badly to protest. In the weeks Jonah had come to the farm, he'd started to fill out. He no longer looked starved. His ivory skin was smooth and perfect. Cole wanted to run his tongue across Jonah's chest, to lap at his tight nipples, and taste the pre-cum glistening on the tip of his cock.

"On the bed like I told you." Jonah's voice was hard, so different from usual.

A jolt of pure need burned through Cole. He didn't hesitate this time. He stretched out on his back on the bed, folded his hands over his stomach and stared at Jonah, challenging him to take the next step.

Jonah climbed on the bed and knelt between Cole's legs. He took Cole's hands in his and kissed his knuckles tenderly. Cole shuddered as if Jonah had sent electric current through him.

Jonah laced their fingers together and pushed Cole's hands up over his head, pinning him down as he rose over him. "Do you still feel different?"

Cole forced himself to consider what he was feeling beyond the driving desire to come. When his wolf was snarling inside him, he wouldn't have submitted. He would have fought Jonah's hold. Now all he felt was a stubborn desire to protest his position, no animal rage needing to be free. He nodded.

"All that rage and ferocity is in your wolf now. You can summon it if you want to, but you can also let go of the animal and submit to pleasure." As Jonah spoke, he leaned down more, bringing his lips so close to Cole's that Cole could feel the heat of his breath. Jonah's cock pressed against Cole's. Cole arched up, needing the friction, needing to feel hard flesh touching his.

But Jonah pulled back. "Not yet. We're going to go slow."

Cole glared at him. "No."

Jonah raised a brow. "Think you can't take it?"

Cole snarled. "Bastard. I can take anything you give."

"We'll see." Jonah's lips ghosted over Cole's then he flicked his tongue across them, giving nothing but a tease.

Cole strained, reaching for more but Jonah sat back laughing. He wanted those lips but he wasn't going to fight. No way in hell was Jonah going to break him.

Jonah slid back. The fine hair on his lower abdomen teased Cole's cock, making him bite his lip to hold in a moan. Jonah gave teasing kisses to Cole's nipples before pressing his lips firmly right over Cole's heart. He worked his way down with lips and tongue, never giving Cole as much attention or pressure as he craved.

When he reached Cole's cock, he blew a warm breath along the length. So close. Cole wanted to grab Jonah's head and push his cock between his teasing lips. A few days ago, his wolf would have forced him to. Growling and snarling, he would have taken hold of Jonah, pinned him down, and fucked him through the mattress. Jonah would have loved it, but Cole would have been afraid he'd lose his mind.

Now he just wanted Jonah with all of a man's need rather than a wolf's. He wanted those sweet lips around his cock. He wanted to see Jonah's eye light up as he swallowed him down. He sank his teeth into his lower lip to keep from begging.

Jonah kissed Cole's balls softly and teased his inner thighs with featherlight caresses. "Pull your legs up and hold them there." His commanding tone was at odds with the soft touches that were all he was willing to give.

Cole glared at him.

Jonah raised a brow and glared back.

Cole tested him by refusing to move. Jonah slapped his ass hard, driving a grunt from him.

"Damn it, Jonah."

He slapped Cole again. Hot pain bloomed across his ass. He couldn't decide if he hated it or loved it, but he pulled his legs up like Jonah wanted. He was exposed, vulnerable. His heart beat too fast. He couldn't get enough air. "Jonah." The word escaped before he could stop it.

Jonah laid his hand on Cole's thigh. "I'm right here."

Cole relaxed. Jonah would take care of him.

Jonah gave the same teasing attention to Cole's ass that he'd given the rest of his body. First with his fingers caressing lightly over Cole's hole, circling it. Then his mouth was there, and Cole couldn't stop himself from begging. "Please. Jonah, please."

"What do you need?" Jonah asked licking him between each word.

"You."

Jonah pushed his tongue into Cole, making him cry out. He alternated stabbing thrusts of his tongue and long firm licks. Then he sat back. "What do you need from me?'

"Please." Cole didn't want to say any more.

Jonah rose on his knees and took hold of his cock. He worked himself in long slow strokes. "Do you need this?" He looked down at his thick, hard flesh.

Cole nodded.

"Tell me."

"Damn it, Jonah."

"Tell me what you want." Jonah's hand moved faster. His breathing grew ragged.

Oh, fuck. He won't come, will he? He won't come before he buries that hot cock in my ass. "Fuck me."

Jonah smiled. "You want my cock inside you."

"Yes, please."

"Good, because I want to fuck you. I want to show you just how well a stallion can use you."

"Oh. My. God." Cole couldn't believe the intensity of need Jonah stirred in him.

Jonah grinned as he reached for the lube and got himself ready. He pushed a lubed finger past the tight muscle guarding Cole's entrance, gasping when Cole relaxed enough to let him in. He moaned as he worked the digit in and out slowly. "So tight, so hot."

"More." Cole didn't want to wait. He wanted Jonah inside him right then. He didn't give a damn about prep, didn't care if it hurt.

Jonah added a second finger and worked them faster. Cole's ass burned, but he only wanted more. He worked himself against Jonah as much as he could with his legs pinned between them.

Jonah slapped his ass. "Be still."

"Jonah!" A bit of the wolf's growl crept in, but Cole was in complete control of it. He wanted Jonah to hear his wolf, to remember what he was. Because he wasn't going to wait forever. If Jonah didn't get on with it, Cole would take what he needed.

"I don't want to hurt you." Jonah slowly slid his fingers out of Cole's body as he spoke.

"I don't fucking care."

Jonah raised a brow. He slid his hands up Cole's legs until he circled Cole's ankles and draped his legs over his shoulders. "Arms above your head."

Cole growled. He had been pushed as far as he would go.

Jonah took his cock in his hand and brushed it over Cole's anus. "Arms over your head, or we're not going any further."

Cole scowled at him. "You need this as bad as I do."

Jonah scowled back. "I can be just as fucking stubborn as you, Cole Wilder."

"Bastard." Cole reached up and grabbed the headboard. Jonah pushed at his entrance.

Cole gasped. *Fuck!* Jonah was huge. He wasn't sure this was going to work.

"Never had a stallion inside you?"

"Fuck no. I —"

His words were cut off by Jonah pushing forward again, impaling him on his massive cock. He couldn't breathe. He'd never imagined feeling so fucking full.

"Cole, you with me?"

"Yeah. Want you." His cock throbbed with need despite the pain.

"Tell me if you need me to stop."

He snarled. "No stopping."

Jonah rolled his eyes.

Just when Cole thought he might have to give in and ask Jonah to give him a minute to adjust, Jonah altered his angle. His cock brushed Cole's prostate. Cole jerked and whimpered.

Jonah smiled. "You like that?"

"Fuck yeah."

He pulled back and worked over the same spot again.

"Jonah!" Cole ignored the desperation in his voice. All he cared about was the burning ecstasy Jonah was giving him.

Jonah wrapped a hand around Cole's cock, stroking him as he pushed in farther, stretching Cole even more.

"Give me all of it," Cole panted.

Jonah grabbed Cole's hips, dragging him the rest of the way onto his cock. Cole gasped as Jonah's thighs touched his ass. He thought Jonah might have split him in two, but he didn't care. All he wanted was for Jonah to fuck him hard, show him no mercy. "Fuck me." The words came out in his low, threatening wolf's voice.

Jonah laughed. "Isn't that what I'm doing?"

Cole snarled. "Hard and fast. Right fucking now."

Jonah pulled out slowly. "Turn over."

Cole did as Jonah asked, praying he was going to get the fucking he needed. Jonah pushed back in even slower than before.

"Harder."

Jonah slapped his ass. "I'm controlling this."

Cole started to protest again, but Jonah flexed his cock deep inside Cole, making him see stars. He pushed back, trying to get more of Jonah's fat cock inside him.

Jonah stroked Cole's cock slowly. "So needy. But you *can* do this, can't you? You *can* let me have control."

"Fuck you." A growl rumbled deep in his chest.

"I'm sure you will later. I bet you'll tear my ass up for doing this to you. In fact, I'm counting on it."

Jonah's words were driving him wild. Jonah's hand stroked him faster. "Jonah, I'm …"

"Oh yeah, come for me."

And Cole did, just like that. Jonah's words brought him over, and his load shot so hard, it struck his chin. Jonah milked Cole's cock while pounding his ass with the hard rhythm Cole had begged for.

When Cole was totally spent, Jonah grabbed Cole's hip with his cum-slick hand and pulled him back hard, stretching him impossibly. "I fucking love you, do you know that?"

"Yes!" Cole cried.

"I… oh, fuck… Cole!"' Jonah's muscles spasmed as he came, driving against Cole in staccato thrusts.

Chapter 12

Cole and Jonah no longer believed Nathan could drive them apart, but the attacks on the farm continued. Someone slashed the tires on two of the farm trucks. Cut brake lines resulted in a minor accident when Danielle drove into town one afternoon. She was lucky. The wreck could have been much more serious.

One morning, they woke up to find several of their chickens slaughtered and "Die Fags" written in blood on the side of the barn. Jonah stared, frozen in place. "They say we're immoral," he said in a voice so quiet it gave Cole chills.

Cole kicked the barn door so hard he split the wood. Then he changed form and raced through the pastures to let off steam, scaring the shit out of the few horses he passed.

The only thing that got him through all the attacks was having Jonah by his side. Every time Cole touched Jonah, even just a brush of a hand, love and lust rushed through him making him smile. How did he get so lucky?

A few days after the attack on the chickens, they got good news. Sheriff Trent called to let them know he'd gotten a confession out of the man who'd bought Jonah from his brother. He'd charged Nathan with kidnapping, assault, and trafficking in shifters. Unfortunately, Nathan was released on bail a few days later.

Cole and Jonah braced themselves for a full-scale attack. Instead, even the flack they took in town slowed down. But Cole waited for a—possibly literal—bomb to drop.

A week after Nathan's release, Cole was making sandwiches. Jonah came in and plopped down at the table. He ran his hands through his hair and when he looked at Cole, he knew something was wrong.

Jonah set his phone on the table, looking as if he were afraid to touch it. "Nathan called me."

Cole fought the urge to throw the sandwich he was holding. "What did he say?" *Please don't let him have shaken Jonah's confidence.*

"He wants a chance to talk to me. He asked me to come see him tomorrow."

Now Cole knew why there'd been no more attacks. "Fucking bastard called off his dogs. He thinks he'll get you to drop the charges."

"Probably, but I think we should hear him out. We need to know what he's planning."

"I know what he's planning. He's going to do his best to bully you into saying you made the whole story up or I made it up and convinced you it was true."

"Cole. I need to do this. I need to confront him."

Cole sighed. Jonah was right. Knowing he could stand up to his brother was important to him. He wouldn't be able to move past what his family had done to him if he didn't. But what if Nathan had something even more sinister in mind? They had proof Nathan wanted them dead. "What if he's setting a trap for us?"

Jonah shook his head. "It's possible, but Nathan is sure he's right. He actually believes he can convince me he acted in my best interest. He still thinks he can turn me straight or at least get me out of town, maybe get rid of you too."

"Did he tell you that?" The idea of Jonah having to listen to his brother telling him he was sick and trying to convince him he could be healed turned Cole's stomach. He set his sandwich down on the counter, no longer hungry.

Jonah looked down, his fingers tracing a stain on the wooden table. "Yeah. He said if I'd come home, he'd get me some help so I could learn to like women."

Cole pounded the counter with his fist. "Fucking bastard. Don't you listen to a word he says. There is nothing wrong with you."

"I know, but—"

Cole knelt by Jonah's chair and took Jonah's face in his hands. "No buts. I love you. You are perfect exactly as you are. I will not lose you because your brother, a man who would force you to live as an animal, sell you to someone who would torture you, cut open a chicken and write with her blood, tells you you're not well. He's evil, Jonah, and he's going to pay for what he's done."

Jonah nodded. "I need to know I can face him without giving in. I need to tell him what I think of how he's treated me."

Cole's heart pounded. He didn't want to agree to this. "OK, but you're not going alone."

Jonah smiled. "I don't want to. I need to confront Nathan, but I also need you there, backing me up. If that makes me weak—"

"Never. It makes you smart. The man wants you dead. You'd be a fool to go see him alone."

"My mom will be there. Do you really think my mom—" His voice broke off in a sob.

Cole pulled Jonah against him. "I don't know if she'd stop him. I just don't know. I wish I did." Cole held Jonah tightly, rubbing a hand up and down his back, wanting to take all the pain, wanting to kill every one of the fucking assholes who'd ever criticized Jonah, ever taught him he wasn't worthy of love, that he needed to change. He was fucking perfect just like he was.

"We should tell Trent we're going to be there."

"Nathan's going to be pissed. He wants this to be family only."

"Fuck what Nathan wants. He gave up the right to dictate anything the moment he tried to kill you. We'd be dumb as hell not to protect ourselves."

Jonah sighed and pulled away. "What if I can't do this? Did you hear me just now? Still worried about what Nathan will think. I've been fucking programmed to keep him happy, keep him from…" Jonah's voice trailed off. He looked lost in memories, the kind that gave him nightmares.

"Keep him from what? God, Jonah did he hurt you even before he sent you away?"

Jonah looked away. "Not Nathan. He likes others to do his dirty work. I can't believe he had the nerve to be the one to drug me that night."

Cole grabbed Jonah, squeezing his biceps and he forced Jonah to look at him. "Who hurt you?"

Jonah looked down.

"Damn it, Jonah. Tell me."

"Anytime I did something Nathan thought was immoral, like changing into horse form, he would tell our stepdad. He'd get Preacher Ted to discipline me. Mama said she didn't like it, but he told her it was the only way to get the sin out of me. Ted usually spanked me or hit me, but once he used a horsewhip.

"A few months later, Nathan caught me kissing my friend's cousin. He was visiting for the holidays and we hit it off. He stopped by to tell me good-bye before he left town. He kissed me and Nathan walked in. I don't think my friend realized how homophobic my family is. I had to stop Nathan from laying into him. And then…"

Jonah stopped. He looked stricken.

The thought of how scared he must have been sickened Cole. He cupped Jonah's face between his hands and kissed him gently. "Nothing you tell me will change how I feel about you."

Tears streaked down Jonah's cheeks. "Nathan told Mama what had happened. She told him to just pray for me, but he couldn't wait to tell Preacher Ted. Nathan called him, and he came rushing home. Mama looked terrified when he stormed in the door, but he pushed her out of the way and grabbed me.

He dragged me out to the barn and told me he knew my filthy secret."

Cole fought the nausea swimming in his stomach. He didn't want to hear what happened next.

"He threw me against the wall. I fell to my knees in the hay, stunned. I heard him unbuckling his belt. I thought he was going to beat me with it. It wouldn't have been the first time, but when I looked up, he was opening his pants. He pulled his cock out and started stroking it."

Jonah shuddered. "I'll never forget what he said. 'You like sucking cock, boy? That's what your brother says. Get down on your knees, you fucking fag, and show me what you've been up to.'"

"Jonah. Oh, God, Jonah. I'm so sorry." Cole didn't know what to say. His stomach roiled. How could anyone do this to his own stepson? Why didn't his mama stop the man?

Cole squeezed Jonah's hand, but he kept going with his story as if he were lost in the memory. "I told him no, and he backhanded me. He was jerking off the whole time, getting off on insulting me. He grabbed my chin and held me in place while he rubbed his cock on my face. I thought I was going to puke all over him. I had to get away so I grabbed his balls and twisted them. He let go of me as he howled in pain. I shoved him. He hit his head against a post and slumped to the ground."

Cole sucked in a breath. "That was the night he died."

Jonah nodded. "The official cause of death was heart attack. I still don't know if Nathan bribed them to say that or not. Maybe the shock of my standing up for myself did him in, but I know he was alive when I pushed him."

Rage and sadness squeezed Cole's chest. "Nathan let him get away with it. He knows what Ted did, and he still talks about him like he was God's right hand man."

"You think he was going to admit his brother's gay, and the preacher he idolized tried to rape him?"

"No decent person could still idolize someone after that, and your sexual orientation makes no difference. Gay or straight, this man attacked you, and your big brother kept you from talking about it."

Tears ran down Jonah's cheeks. "H-he said it was my fault, that I'd corrupted Ted from his walk with God. He said I had demons in me, and he was going to find a way to get them out."

"My God, you came to me not long after that. I remember. Your stepfather had only been dead for a few months when you asked me for a job."

"I wanted to tell you, but I couldn't." Jonah broke down, sobbing, and Cole held him until the outpouring of grief passed.

"Nathan will pay for everything he's done. No matter what I have to do, he will not walk away from this."

Jonah shook his head. "Don't risk yourself to get to him. I want a chance to be happy with you."

Cole looked into Jonah's beautiful eyes, and his chest tightened painfully. "Why? Why do you still want me after I left you vulnerable to that disgusting excuse for a family?"

Jonah lifted Cole's hands and kissed them. "You rescued me in the end. That's all that matters."

"Damn right this is the end. Nathan is never going to hurt you again."

Jonah nodded. "But I have to be the one to tell him I'm not going to stop until justice is done. You have to back down and let me do this. I need to be more than just some stray you've taken in because I'm too weak to care for myself."

"I've never thought of you like that, but if I'd stood up for you a year ago, we wouldn't be here now."

"If I'd stood up for myself, I would have left the first time Ted hit me."

"My God, Jonah, you were what, fifteen when it started? How could you be expected to know what to do?"

"I was old enough to get away. I could work. I could've found a farm to take me with my gift for talking to horses."

"You could have had a job here if I hadn't been such a fool."

Jonah made a low noise between a growl and a snort. "Don't say that again. You had no reason to hire me. I was the fool. I was in love with you. I thought…"

"You thought I'd save you, and I should have." Pain cut through Cole like a knife. How could he ever forgive himself?

"But if you had, you'd still be saving me, protecting me. I would never have had to grow up, and this relationship wouldn't have worked. Either

I'd have resented you for telling me what to do, or you'd have gotten tired of taking care of a kid."

"I would never…"

Jonah raised his brows.

Cole hated that he was right. "Fine."

"You do see me as an equal, right? Not some kid you're taking care of?"

Anger burned in Cole. How could Jonah ask that now? "Of course I do. You taught me how to accept my wolf and reconcile all the anger inside me. No kid could do that."

Jonah smiled. "Damn right."

Cole grabbed the front of Jonah's shirt and pulled him in for a kiss. He poured all his desperation, his conflict, his desire to protect and love into Jonah. When he finally let go, Jonah brushed his cheek with the back of his knuckles. "I forgive you for not hiring me."

Cole's heart swelled. Those simple words released him. He hadn't realized how badly he needed that absolution. "Thank you."

Jonah smiled at him. Love washed over him, renewing him. "We *will* win this."

Chapter 13

Jonah knocked at the door of his childhood home. His mother answered the door. Her eyes were red and puffy, her skin sallow. "I'm glad you've come home, Jonah."

He looked like he wasn't sure how to respond. Did she think he'd come home to stay, to let them try to brainwash him again? Cole hoped to hell not. From the stories Jonah had told about his childhood, his mother had been strict, set in her beliefs about the sinfulness of using their animal forms, but she'd loved him, cared for him, made him feel like he was a part of the family until Preacher Ted had come to take over their church and starting raining hellfire on anyone who thought differently from him.

"You best come inside," Mrs Marks said, her voice shaky.

"Mama—" Jonah laid a hand on her arm.

She laid her hand over his, but she turned away. "Nathan's waiting."

Cole started to say if Jonah wanted to talk to her, Nathan could damn well wait, but she glared at him. "You're not welcome here."

"Jonah's not talking to Nathan alone. If he goes in, I go in."

She stood her ground. "This is a family matter."

"When a family member tries to kill another, they give up the right to call themselves family. I'm Jonah's family now, and I'm not leaving."

"Nathan said—"

"Mama, for once, would you listen to me instead of Nathan? You can still think for yourself, can't you?"

She swayed backward like he'd slapped her. "Jonah!"

"Goddamn it, Mama, Nathan drugged me and sold me. I ended up beaten and half-starved. I'll have scars for the rest of my life." Jonah pulled up his shirt, showing her the scars on his back.

She looked at the floor. "Jonah, please."

"I know you don't want me to be gay, but Cole loves me. He wants to protect me. How can that be wrong and leaving me for dead be right?"

Mrs Marks started to speak, but Jonah didn't give her a chance. "How can it be OK for Nathan to send his friends to shoot me? How the fuck could you stand by and watch Nathan and that damn preacher abuse me? How could you?"

She stared at Jonah with tears in her eyes. She didn't say anything in her defense, but she didn't apologize either.

Jonah brushed past her and Cole followed. Nathan was in the den, standing by the wood stove, his back to them. Cole longed to pull out his pistol and shoot the bastard, but he wouldn't shoot a man in the back, not even scum like Nathan.

Nathan turned around, a smirk on his face. "I didn't think you'd be sensible enough to come."

Jonah snorted, sounding like Demon. "What do you want?"

Nathan took a step toward Jonah. Cole laid a hand on the butt of his gun. "Stay back and keep your hands where I can see them."

Nathan glared at him, showing no apprehension. "You weren't invited."

"I'm not about to let Jonah come near you without backup."

"Are you afraid I'll convince him to repent his sins? Then you won't have a little whore to serve you."

Cole's wolf stirred, and he wanted to let the beast free. He saw himself leaping across the room and pinning Nathan.

Jonah laid a hand on his arm. "He's not worth it."

Cole looked at Jonah, letting the sight of his lover pull him back into his human form. Jonah smiled, sensing that Cole was backing down. Cole's chest tightened as he saw love on Jonah's face. Jonah turned back to his brother. "You asked me here to talk, so talk."

Nathan eyed Jonah like he was assessing him, figuring out the best way to manipulate him. "Here's the thing. We both know you're not going to win this case. So a shady horse dealer is willing to say he purchased a horse from me, so what? Do you really think a man of my standing won't be able to easily discredit him?"

"It'll be harder to discredit DNA evidence. That horse he bought was me. We have the blood samples to prove it."

"So my freak brother decided to live as a horse for a year. That's not got a damn thing to do with me. You need to drop the charges before you make a fool of yourself."

Cole tensed. Nathan was more right than he wanted to admit. The law was prejudiced against shifters anyway, and when you added the fact Jonah was gay, a lawyer would be hard-pressed to find a jury around here that would credit anything he said.

But Jonah didn't back down. "If you're so damn sure you're going to win, what difference does it make?"

Nathan looked at Jonah the way he would a big nasty bug. "I don't want our family's good name mixed up in this. It's disgusting the way you've let this fag brainwash you and make you forsake your own family."

Jonah made the low growling snort that signaled he was pissed as hell. If he had been in horse form, Cole would have expected him to kick. "You deserve to be forsaken. You've belittled me my whole life, encouraged your friends to abuse me, and then… you let our stepfather —"

Nathan stepped forward. Cole rested his hand on his gun, ready to draw.

"Don't you dare," Nathan roared.

"He tried to rape me, Nathan, tried to fucking rape me, and your reaction was to cover it up, threaten me, and then kidnap me. Is that how a man of God acts? Is that how God commands you to solve your problems?"

"You killed him." Nathan advanced another step.

Cole pulled his gun and aimed it at Nathan's head. "Don't move."

Neither man seemed to hear him.

"I fought back," Jonah screamed. "For once in my life, I fought back, and I'm fighting now. I won't let this go. You're going to rot in prison for what you've done to me."

Nathan drew himself up to his full height and tried to regain his composure. He gave Cole a disdainful look, acting unconcerned about the gun still trained on him. Cole's finger itched to pull the trigger. If Nathan took one step out of line, if he so much as touched Jonah, Cole would take him down.

Nathan looked back at his brother. "Aren't you tired of being his bitch?"

"I love Cole, but that's something you can't understand. You've based your life on hate."

"You're pathetic. You really believe he loves you, don't you? He's just using you. He needs somewhere to stick his dick, and you're willing to offer your ass."

Jonah punched Nathan, knocking him back. Nathan reached back to brace himself and laid his hand against the side of the wood stove. He screamed. "You made me burn my hand, you whoring bastard!" He curled in on himself, cradling his hand against his chest.

Cole holstered his gun, but neither Jonah nor Cole made a move to help Nathan.

"Goddamn it, get me some ice!" Nathan screamed.

"There's no need to take the Lord's name in vain," his mother said, her voice flat. She stepped out from the shadows of the doorway. Cole had been so focused on Nathan and Jonah he hadn't realized she was there.

Jonah snorted. "I guess you're not so righteous when you're the one in pain."

"Somebody help me," Nathan whined.

His mother just glared at him. "Is what he said true, Nathan? Did Ted force himself on Jonah?"

Nathan looked like he might throw up.

Before anyone answered, the doorbell rang.

Jonah's mother went to answer it, and a few seconds later, Sheriff Trent walked in. Jonah's mother followed him, carrying a square wooden box. When Nathan saw it, the last bit of color drained from his face. "Mama, what are you doing with that?"

"What I should have done a year ago, giving it to the authorities."

"It's nothing, Mama."

"The hell it's nothing. It's the drug you used on your brother."

"He's a sinner, Mama. He doesn't belong here."

"I don't like his lifestyle, and I pray for him every night. But I still love him, and I never wanted to get rid of him."

"I thought you loved *me*." Nathan looked stricken as if she'd slapped him.

"I do. I pray for you too, Nathan, but I can't hide this anymore, not what you did to Jonah, or anything else."

Nathan's eyes widened. "You knew? About Preacher Ted?"

Tears ran down her cheeks. "I never knew the details, but when he went out to the barn with Jonah, there was lust on his face. It wasn't right, wasn't natural."

"He did it." Nathan pointed to Jonah. "He turned Ted away from God, tempted him with his sick ways."

"Mama, I did my best to stay out of his way," Jonah said. "You know that. I never wanted anything to do with him, and I sure as hell didn't want him touching me."

His mother nodded. "I know, Jonah. That is one thing I do know."

Sheriff Trent took the box from her. "Nathan, I need to ask you some questions."

Nathan glared at him. "Not now."

"I can bring you in on an illegal possession charge, or you can talk to me here."

"I've never seen that box before."

Trent raised a brow. "Really? That's not what you indicated earlier."

Nathan waved his good hand toward Jonah and Cole. "They've gotten to Mama. Now she's trying to set me up, but God will save me."

His mother shook her head. "You turned your back on God a long time ago. We both did. Ted wasn't a man of God. He was a bully who wanted power any way he could get it."

"No. It's Jonah's fault. God wants him punished."

"God wants Jonah to repent of his sins, but he doesn't want to harm him, just to love him." Tears rolled down Mrs Marks's face.

Nathan turned away. His shoulders shook as he sobbed. Cole almost felt sorry for him, but then without warning, Nathan grabbed the poker and turned.

His face contorted with rage. He was the monster Cole imagined him to be. He swung for Jonah's head and missed, making a dent in the floor. Screaming, he lifted the poker and went after Jonah again. The second blow missed as Jonah scrambled out of the way.

"No!" Cole screamed. He and Trent drew their guns.

"Put the poker down, or I'll be forced to shoot," Trent yelled. Nathan had the strength of a shifter. Trent had no chance of restraining him by other means.

The next seconds seemed to pass in slow motion. Jonah stumbled. He ducked and covered his head. Nathan slammed the poker down, hitting him on the shoulder, the force of the blow knocking him to the floor.

Nathan raised his weapon again. "You're going to die. Now!"

The Sheriff got a shot off at nearly the same time as Cole. Both bullets hit Nathan in the chest. Red bloomed on the front of his shirt, and he dropped to his knees gasping for breath.

Cole rushed to Jonah. He heard the sheriff call for an ambulance, as he helped Jonah sit up. "I'm so sorry. I didn't see that coming."

"It's OK. We stopped him." Jonah's voice was soft, filled with pain, but he smiled at Cole.

Cole shuddered as he thought about what could have happened if Nathan had made contact with Jonah's head. "Are you really OK?"

Jonah nodded. "Yeah. Help me get outside where I can shift. That'll help me heal faster."

Cole scooped Jonah up in his arms.

Jonah spluttered. "I meant help me to my feet."

"Hush. There's no way I'm letting you walk."

"Where are you going?" Trent asked. "Jonah needs to see a doctor."

Cole kept walking. "Outside so he can shift."

"Mama," Jonah called as they reached the door. Sweat dripped down his face, and his voice was barely audible. Cole hated knowing he was in so much pain.

Mrs Marks knelt by Nathan where he lay on the floor, his face gray, his eyes dull. When she looked up, Cole saw confusion and resentment in her eyes. "Leave us in peace."

"If Nathan shifts, he'll be OK," Jonah said, ignoring her.

"No." Nathan whispered the word, a sick gurgling coming from his chest. One of the bullets must have punctured a lung.

"Shifting will repair most of the damage. It's your best chance."

Jonah's mother turned to her older son. "Nathan, do what he says."

"No. Not… an… animal."

"Stubborn bastard." Cole walked out with Jonah, not about to let him suffer any longer because his brother hated himself so much he'd rather risk death than be who he was born to be.

Chapter 14

Despite the odds, Nathan survived his wounds. He made a formal confession, and his sentencing was scheduled for the following week when the doctors predicted he would be able to leave the hospital. His mother stayed at his bedside, but she refused to let anyone from the church visit him. Cole wondered how many of the members had known what Preacher Ted was really like.

Jonah had talked to his mother once. She told him she would keep praying for him and asked for his forgiveness. He gave it and told her he appreciated her prayers, but he was happy with who he was and didn't believe God wanted him to change.

Cole hoped someday she'd come to accept him and Jonah for who they were, but for now they had each other, the farm, and a wonderful crew of people who cared about them. That was more than most men were blessed with.

Cole pitched straw into the last stall in the barn. Next on his list of chores was checking on a repair to one of the fences that had been cut weeks before. The quick fix they'd done had failed, and Shep wanted Cole to make sure it looked like the repair he'd done would hold.

As he put his tools away, he smelled Jonah's bright, citrusy scent. Jonah had been working on an expansion of the tack room. Cole heard Jonah's boots slap against the floor of the barn. He took a deep breath. Jonah smelled like sweat and hard work, and Cole's cock responded instantly. He hung up the pitchfork and turned to face his lover.

"What're you up to?" Jonah asked.

"Getting ready to inspect the section of fence Shep's been working on."

"You want some help?"

"Hell, yeah." He always wanted Jonah with him, but how would he keep his mind on work now that he was horny as hell?

Jonah grinned. "I thought you might."

"Just what kind of help do you intend to give?"

Jonah titled his head to one side like he was considering the question. "What kind do you need?"

Cole reached for Jonah, grabbed him by the back of the neck and pulled him in for a rough tangle of tongues, teeth, and raw need. When Cole moved away to catch his breath, Jonah spread kisses over his jaw, circled his ear with his tongue and whispered, "I want you to ride me."

Cole wanted that too. He was rock hard, and his cock begged to be released from his jeans. Duty warred with his need for pleasure. "Mmm, sounds wonderful."

Jonah smiled. "I mean I want you to ride my horse form."

Cole stared at Jonah. Most shifters never let humans use them the way they did their animal counterparts. "Are you sure?"

Jonah nodded. "For a horse shifter, letting a human ride us is the ultimate sign of trust and respect. I've never willingly accepted a rider, only had them forced on me while I was trapped in horse form. I want to feel someone on my back who cares about me."

"Snowdrop and Lady tolerate me. I can ride a few of the other horses if I use a firm hand. The rest won't have anything to do with me. I've never had the experience of feeling like I was one with my horse. I didn't think it was possible for a wolf."

Jonah grinned. "It's possible with me."

Cole squeezed Jonah's hand. "Thank you."

Jonah backed away. He stripped and laid his clothes aside. The air around him shimmered as he became Demon. Cole walked out of the barn and Demon followed, lining himself up perfectly with the mounting block. Cole grabbed hold of Demon's mane and lifted himself onto his back. Cole patted his neck. "Take us to the south pasture, baby. I'm in the mood for a fast, hard ride."

Demon whinnied and took off. Cole lay over his neck, clinging to his mane with his hands. Once they reached open pasture, Demon sped to a full gallop. When they came to a fence, he jumped it neatly.

Cole's heart raced and adrenaline pumped through his body. There was no struggle, no resistance like with other horses. He and Demon moved as one. Demon's hooves ate up the ground as they prepared to jump another fence. Demon's body bunched and then stretched under him, perfectly made for jumping. Cole didn't think he'd ever been happier. What he and Jonah had went beyond friendship, beyond family. True love, the deepest bond a man could feel. He might be a sappy bastard for saying so, but he loved Jonah too much to care.

When they reached their destination, horse and rider were both winded. Cole dismounted and Jonah shifted back to human form. Cole no longer gave a damn about fences.

"Jonah." The word was low and breathy with need. Cole reached for his lover, but Jonah retreated, laughing.

"You have a fence to inspect, Mr Wilder. I'm just your transportation."

"The fuck you are." Cole growled.

"Inspect the fence, and we'll see about what else I can be."

"I want you now."

Jonah shifted back to horse form.

"Goddamn it! I'll make you pay for that."

Jonah snorted.

Cole turned to face the fence. *How can I concentrate with my cock aching? Stubborn stallion.*

He forced himself to look at the fence, knowing instinctively Jonah would be able to tell if he half-assed the job. Shep had done solid work which was a relief. Now Cole could devote the rest of the day to fucking the hell out of Jonah. They both deserved it.

The wolf inside him agreed, but he wanted a run almost as badly as a fuck. Cole turned to face Demon. "Think you can outrun a wolf?"

Demon tossed his head and snorted. Cole smiled. Driving into Jonah after they worked themselves up with a good chase would feel divine.

The weather was even warm enough for a dip in the creek afterward.

Cole stripped quickly, not wanting to rip any more clothes, then he shifted, and the race was on. He chased his stallion over the next two fields. Demon was running right for the spot where he'd gone when Cole thought he was running away. Instinctively, Cole knew that was the finish line.

His heart pounded as his paws hit the ground. Hunger and need, sexual but also deeper, thrummed through him. He sped up. So did Demon, but Cole could catch him.

His muscles stretched, and his feet pushed off the ground. He leaped so high he was almost flying. When he caught Jonah, he wasn't going to give him any mercy. Jonah was prey, and he was Cole's for the taking.

They neared the spot Jonah sought. Cole put on a burst of speed. His wolf was confident. He hadn't needed to push himself, but now it was time to capture his man. *His. Oh hell, yes.* He leaped, jaw closing around Demon's neck, teeth pricking but not doing real damage. They crashed to the ground, both shifting as they hit. Jonah rolled under him, and they ground against each other.

Cole needed to fuse himself to Jonah, to taste, touch, bite. Unlike in the early days of their relationship, he wasn't worried he'd actually hurt Jonah, but he'd caught Jonah, and he was going to keep him.

He flipped Jonah over onto all fours. Face-to-face was nice and sweet, but right now he needed a deep, hard animal fuck.

"Lube. Tree." Jonah gasped.

"What?"

"In there." Jonah pointed at the tree they'd fucked by weeks before. "There's lube and water and…"

What the fuck is he talking about? "Don't move." Cole walked to the tree and reached into the hole at the base. Sure enough he found a bag containing lube, water bottles, snacks, and a blanket. "You planned this."

Jonah looked back at Cole with a cheeky grin. He shook his ass in invitation.

Cole growled. He popped the top on the lube and greased his fingers. He pushed one into Jonah who worked himself on it eagerly. He quickly added another.

"Don't wanna wait." Jonah gasped.

"Me either, but—"

"I'm a stallion. I won't break."

"Jonah, I—"

"Fuck me, Cole."

Cole couldn't deny either of them a second longer. He slicked his cock then pulled Jonah's ass cheeks apart and pushed into him. Jonah tensed.

"You OK?"

"Don't stop."

Cole pushed forward slowly, shuddering as Jonah's tight heat gripped him. "So good."

"Oh, yeah. I—" Jonah's voice caught.

Cole forced himself to stop, but Jonah pushed back, taking him deeper. Cole thrust until he was all the way in. "Can't… go… slow."

"Please," Jonah groaned.

Cole hoped Jonah was begging for more, because he was way beyond stopping. He pulled out and drove back in. Jonah cried out, struggling against Cole's hold on his hips. Cole worked Jonah harder and harder until they were both panting, babbling, begging, striving for that burst of pleasure that would release them from their desperate need.

Next time Cole would go slow. Next time he would use some finesse and show Jonah how much he loved him, but right then his world narrowed to pounding, driving need.

So close. So damn close. Possession. Want. Need. Mine. The words echoed in Cole's head. His wolf growled in agreement. Then Jonah made a noise like a horse's whinny as climax took him. His muscles squeezed Cole's cock, bringing him over.

Cole slammed into Jonah's ass, filling him with cum. His orgasm went on and on until he thought he'd never come back to Earth. Finally, he stilled, and they both collapsed, bruised, grass-stained, exhausted.

"That was incredible." Jonah smiled at him, catching his breath.

Cole was still thrown off guard by how much he loved Jonah. "Yeah, but someday I'll show you I can be romantic too."

Jonah cupped Cole's cheek and caressed him with his thumb. "I like it when you love me like this, like the animals we are."

Cole's cock was already getting interested again. "Yeah?"

Jonah grinned. "Romantic could be nice, but I need to feel you pound my ass like you did just now."

Cole almost choked. "Jonah, you're fucking perfect."

He laughed. "I try."

"Marry me."

Jonah's eyes widened.

Cole hadn't meant for the words to tumble out so fast. "I know we can't legally here, but—"

"Yes."

Cole's heart banged against his ribs. "Yes?"

"Anywhere, any way you want. Officially or just between us. I'm yours. Now and forever." He straddled Cole and leaned down to kiss him.

"I love you," Cole whispered against Jonah's mouth.

Jonah smiled. "I'll never get tired of hearing you say that."

Cole couldn't believe how lucky he was. "Good. Because I plan to say it a lot."

The End

Author Bio

Silvia Violet writes erotic romance and erotica in a variety of genres including sci fi, paranormal and historical. She can be found haunting coffee shops looking for the darkest, strongest cup of coffee she can find. Once equipped with the needed fuel, she can happily sit for hours pounding away at her laptop. Silvia typically leaves home disguised as a suburban stay-at-home-mom, and other coffee shop patrons tend to ask her hilarious questions like "Do you write children's books?" She loves watching the looks on their faces when they learn what she's actually up to.

When not writing, Silvia enjoys baking sinful chocolate treats, exploring new styles of cooking, and reading children's books to her wickedly smart offspring.

Website:
http://silviaviolet.com

Facebook:
http://facebook.com/silvia.violet

Twitter:
http://twitter.com/Silvia_Violet

For a list of Silvia's available titles:
http://silviaviolet.com/books

Wild R Farm Book 2: Arresting Love is available now.

Here's a sneak peek.

Chapter 1

The crazy cuckoo clock his boss's lover had rescued from the farmhouse attic began to chirp, signaling the start of a new year. Cheers went up from the hands, and Billy watched his boss, farm owner Cole Wilder, pull Jonah to him for a kiss.

Billy took a pull from his beer and tried to make himself look away, but he couldn't keep from staring as Cole staked his claim, seeming to devour his young lover. Jonah gave back as good as he got, and Billy's cock stirred in his pants. The two men were beautiful together.

When Cole finally pulled back, the look on his face made Billy's chest ache. No one could miss seeing Cole's love for Jonah. The two men had a bond that was strong as steel, and Billy was jealous.

Four years ago when he'd been hired as barn manager at Wild R Farm, Billy had developed a crush on Cole, but he'd quickly realized Cole would never see him as more than a friend. He'd accepted that. He treasured their friendship, and he never forgot that Cole had given him a chance when he could have hired someone better educated with years more management experience. But watching Cole and Jonah together made him long to connect with someone. Having a man look at him the way Jonah looked at Cole would be a taste of heaven.

Billy drained the rest of his beer. That line of thinking would do nothing but depress him. He needed to be thankful for what he had. The chance of finding the kind of love Cole and Jonah shared was nearly non-existent. He was starting another year doing a job he loved on a farm where he didn't have to hide the fact that he was gay. Considering he'd been kicked out by his family at seventeen, he'd done a damn fine job of pulling his life together.

It wasn't in his nature to be morose, but he'd be turning thirty this year, and he was getting tired of living in a bunkhouse, no matter how much he enjoyed the company of the hands he shared it with. He was weary of men who wanted nothing more than a hard, rough fuck behind a trailer at a horse show. He wanted a home and someone to share it with. Age must be making him soft.

He stepped onto the farmhouse porch and took a breath of the chilly night air. He shivered, but he'd rather be out here than in the crowded house especially in the mood he was in. He leaned against the porch railing and listened to the rush of water in the stream than ran behind the house as he tried to push his depressing thoughts away. One of the horses whinnied, and he wondered if going for a midnight ride would help.

"What you doing out here?" Cole asked, stepping out on the porch and letting the screen door slam behind him.

Billy shrugged. "Just gettin' some fresh air."

Cole frowned. "Are you okay?"

"Yeah, you know I don't like crowds."

Cole snorted. "Me either. I'm about to get rid of everybody since we've rung in the new year. This whole party thing was Jonah's idea. I had a much better plan for the night, but he wouldn't listen."

Billy forced himself to smile. "I'm guessing your plan involved Jonah naked and flat on his back."

Cole grinned. Then he narrowed his eyes and studied Billy. "Are you sure you're all right? You've been grouchy for weeks now."

Billy raised his brows.

"Yeah, yeah. I'm grouchy all the time. I know it." Cole said.

Billy rolled his eyes. "Damn temperamental wolf."

Cole snorted. "I'm better than I used to be, now that I've got Jonah." As soon as those words came out, Cole tensed.

Jonah's brother, Nathan, had kidnapped Jonah, drugged him so he had to remain in horse form then sold him. Fortunately, he'd ended up at Cole's friend's horse sanctuary. As Cole and the rest of the crew at the farm fought for justice for Jonah, Billy ended up in a fist fight with Nathan. In the aftermath, Cole finally realized Billy had hoped for more than friendship between them. Fortunately, Cole hadn't freaked out, but he was still sensitive about talking to Billy about his relationship with Jonah. Billy wished he'd just get over it.

"You're right. Jonah's been good for you." Billy clapped him on the shoulder, and Cole looked his way, tension easing.

"You should take some time off," Cole said. "With planning the addition to the barn and new horses coming in, you've been working non-stop for weeks."

That was true, but when he was working, Billy didn't feel lonely, and he didn't have time to be jealous of Cole. "I don't mind. I'd rather be working with the horses than doing anything else."

Cole frowned. "When was the last time you left the farm?"

Billy shrugged. "I don't know. I went into town a few weeks ago."

Cole raised his brows and glared.

"I'm fine. Really."

"You need a vacation."

Billy shook his head. "I'm happy here. There's nowhere else I want to go."

He'd spent his late teens and early twenties wandering, finding work where he could, never staying anywhere long. Now that he had a place he felt safe and accepted, he never wanted to leave.

Cole leaned closer and sniffed. It had taken Billy a while to get used to Cole's werewolf habits, but now he took such things for granted.

"Something's bothering you," Cole said. "I can smell it."

"I'm just keyed up. It's probably the barn addition. I want to be sure I've got all the details right before we break ground."

"You need to relax," Cole insisted.

Billy scowled. "The last thing I need to is sit around on my ass. You know I can't stay still long."

"Maybe you need to learn how. You're taking a three-day weekend starting next Friday, and I won't listen to any complaints."

Three whole days to think about everything he didn't have instead of concentrating on what was right in his life. "Where the hell do you expect me to go?"

Cole frowned. "I don't know, but I'll figure it out and let you know."

Billy glared at him. "You're not sending me on a trip."

Cole growled. "The hell I'm not. Consider it a bonus."

Look for *Wild R Farm 3* in 2013.